Egg
of the
Dragon

Marked by the Dragon Book 2

RICHARD FIERCE

Dragonfire Press

Cover design by germancreative.

Cover art by Rosauro Ugang

ISBN: 978-1-947329-78-2

CONTENTS

MAP

1

The dragon had been avoiding Mina for days.

At first, she'd thought that the beast had been able to detect her scent, but after doing numerous things to disguise her smell, she'd decided that there had to be another way that he sensed her approach. Perhaps he could see better in the dark than she knew. After all, she had been searching at night.

Today would be different. She could feel it in her bones.

Mina had slipped out of the castle after breakfast, taking Vhan's sword with her. The blasted thing was almost too heavy for her to carry, but it made her feel safe. She laid the blade over her left shoulder, using her own body as leverage. Lord Klodian had been strangely absent, and she suspected it had something to do with the rumors of war circulating around the castle.

The servants had a way of exaggerating what they heard, but with Klodian seemingly preoccupied, it did lend some credence to their words. War or not, it had nothing to do with Mina. The fact that Klodian had ceased his hunts meant that she had more time to find answers to the many questions looming in her mind.

She walked to the stable and set the sword down, placing the pointed end in the dirt and waited for Aram, one of the stable hands, to saddle a horse for her. She would have taken a horse the previous few nights, but she didn't want to arouse attention. There was enough focus on her with the momentous change in status Klodian had given her. He'd named her an advisor, of all things. Mina shook her head as she considered it.

"Where you headed to, my Lady?" Aram asked.

"Just for a ride," Mina replied. "I'll be back in a few hours."

"Tempest here should do the job. She can be a bit stubborn, but she's gentle."

"She'll do fine. Thank you."

Aram led a brown mare out and handed her the reins. The horse nuzzled Mina, and she rubbed her hand along the horse's forehead before offering a quick scratch behind the ears. The mare whinnied and pawed at the ground.

"It seems she likes you," Aram said. He handed her a small bag. "There's a few apples and some oats in there. If you're going to be out past noon, you'll need to give her something to eat. She likes to snack throughout the day."

"I'll be sure to take good care of her. Come on, Tempest."

Mina dragged the sword behind her with one hand and held onto the reins tightly with the other. She walked Tempest to the castle gate, then strapped the sword onto the saddle and did her best to mount the horse without looking too inept. She hadn't ridden a horse on her own since she'd lived on her parent's farm, but she remembered the basics well enough. Once she was firmly seated, she watched and waited.

The Runesmen were doing their morning run around the castle, and she didn't want to accidentally run anyone over. Once the stragglers had passed, Mina clenched her knees against Tempest's sides and flicked the reins. Tempest began a swift trot, and after a few moments of panic, Mina was able to guide the mare in the direction she wanted.

The sensation from the scale in her leg indicated that the dragon was northeast of the castle, the same general area she'd been searching. She rode for half an hour, slightly adjusting Tempest's course as they went. Tall mesas were scattered across the landscape, but she angled the horse toward one in particular. It was tall and wide, but she didn't immediately spot a cave entrance.

"We'll ride around the base and see if we can find one," Mina muttered to herself as much as to Tempest.

It took the better part of an hour, but once she had circled the entire mesa, Mina frowned. The dragon was here, she was certain of it, but there was no cave. She dismounted and fished an apple from the satchel Aram had given her, then fed it to Tempest. The horse took the entire thing in one bite, crunching loudly.

Mina looked up at the mesa. If there was no cave, then the dragon had to be at the top. The idea of scaling the sheer wall to get up there wasn't very appealing, but what other option did she have?

"Can I trust you not to leave me here?" she asked Tempest.

The horse nickered as if replying, and Mina patted its shoulder. She had no idea what awaited her once she finally found the dragon. The beast could easily eat her, for all she knew. She supposed that she must be a little crazy to be seeking a dragon by herself, but if she had brought Klodian on her quest, he would want to kill the dragon and claim its hoard of treasure.

At any other time, Mina would have no qualms with that. But for now, she wanted answers, which meant that she would have to speak with the dragon, not kill it. Speak with a dragon. The thought seemed foolish, but after her encounter with the enormous copper beast, she knew that there was much more about dragons that she didn't know or understand.

Mina retrieved the sword from Tempest's saddle and carried it with her to the mesa wall. It quickly became apparent that she wouldn't be able to carry it while she climbed. The surface of the mesa had enough grooves for her to find foot and handholds, but the added weight and awkwardness of the sword would only hinder her.

She heaved a sigh and set the sword down, propping it against the stone wall. Grabbing a handful of dirt from the ground, she rubbed it between her hands and then began climbing up the wall. Having small fingers ended up benefitting her, and she made quick progress until she reached what she thought was the halfway point.

Her muscles burned with exertion, and her legs began to tremor. She gritted her teeth against the pain, pausing long enough to carefully brush the sweat from each of her hands onto her pants. The sun was high overhead, and without a cloud in the sky, the heat was making her sweat in places she'd rather not think about.

"Almost there," she whispered, though she knew that was a lie.

Still, if she could make herself believe it, perhaps she wouldn't fall to her death. She breathed deeply, trying to calm herself, then continued climbing. Her pace was much slower now, and the higher she climbed, the more pain she felt in her hands. Something sticky was on her fingertips, but she didn't look to confirm if it was blood.

Finally, she reached the top of the mesa. Mina pulled herself over the edge, struggling for a moment. She almost tumbled backward, but she clawed frantically at the rocks and managed to catch herself. Her heart hammered in her chest and she laid on her back with her eyes closed, a thin shield against the sun. After a long moment of rest, she rolled onto her side and looked down at the ground far below. Tempest was nothing more than a tiny brown dot.

Mina forced herself to her feet and turned around to survey her surroundings. The top of the mesa was wide and flat. Patches of desert shrubs, all dull green, littered the surface. The scale in her leg thrummed powerfully, but she didn't see the dragon anywhere. Did they have the ability to camouflage themselves? Or could they perhaps make themselves invisible completely?

As she considered those questions, movement caught her eye. Mina squinted, but it was difficult to see what had moved. She crept forward, wiping droplets of sweat from her brow. Reaching a long line of shrubs, she realized that there was a large depression hidden behind them. Mina stepped into the thorny bushes, spurs grabbing at her clothes.

The indentation sloped down smoothly, and there at the bottom was the dragon. It lay there, basking in the sun, its wings outstretched. She swallowed hard, fighting against the fear that threatened to consume her. She'd finally found him. And now that he was within sight, her carefully crafted plan shattered into pieces.

What was she doing up here? She'd made a terrible mistake. *Blessed Avera,* Mina thought. *This beast will surely kill me.* She was frozen in place, dragon fear slowly taking over her senses. Her mind screamed at her body to turn and run, but her muscles wouldn't—or couldn't—obey. Her lips refused to part and take in air, and her lungs cried out. She fought desperately against the fear and won, gasping in a deep breath.

The dragon's eyes snapped open.

2

Velbridge was the heart of the Dracan Dominion. It was also the seat of power for the High Prince's favored ruler, Lord Kristofel D'Lance.

As Caden navigated the busy streets of the sprawling city, he marveled at the number of people that the place could accommodate. They thronged down every cobbled street, the sight reminding him of how small the Thophate in its entirety was in comparison. Vendor stalls were everywhere, even at the middle of intersections, and the scent of exotic foods filled the air, tempting Caden to see if they tasted as good as they smelled.

Behind the city loomed a castle twice the size of Lord Klodian's, and its dark gray walls stood in stark contrast to all the color that the city presented. This was his new home. It was hard for him to believe that being sent here was a punishment, but his excitement was dampened by the memory of Thais's betrayal. If she had kept her mouth shut, he'd still be in the Thophate with Mina.

There was nothing he could do about it now, though, and he tried not to dwell on it. He held the letter of his transfer in his right hand. He'd found it in the bag of provisions Captain Eduard had given him. Lord Klodian's flowing signature was at the bottom, along with his official seal. Halfway through the journey, Caden had briefly considered giving up his dreams and turning around, but it had only been an idea born of the desert heat. Once he'd reached more forgiving lands, his thoughts returned to normal.

"You there," a vendor called out to him. "You look like you could use a drink. I've got the best ale in all of Dracan. Only a hundred silver for a full barrel."

Caden smiled despite the exorbitant price and continued walking. He was heading for the castle, but navigating the crowded streets was proving to be more of a pain than he'd first thought. He pushed his way through the crowd, receiving a few elbows to the ribs that he doubted were accidental. Eventually, he found a side street that ran parallel to the main one, and he turned onto it and was able to quicken his pace. The castle seemed to grow and stretch the closer he got until he found himself at the gates.

He craned his neck back, trying to take in the view. A group of soldiers standing guard saw him gawking and laughed. Caden cleared his throat and walked confidently over to them.

"Good day," he said. "I've just transferred from the Thophate Dominion. Can one of you show me to the captain?"

"Another transfer, huh? Seems everyone is coming here lately. Stay here, gents. I'll take him."

The man who'd spoken was older than the others, with dull black hair that was beginning to turn silver. He sported a thick handlebar mustache and his face was creased with a few wrinkles. The other guards shrugged and resumed their conversation, and the older man led Caden through the gates and into the courtyard. He walked with a slight limp, but his pace was swift and Caden had trouble keeping up with him.

"What's your name?"

"Caden. Caden Davtyan."

"Well met. I'm Angus. You're from the Thophate, you said?"

"Yes, sir," Caden replied. "I just arrived today."

"I've never been there myself, but I've heard terrible things from some of the merchants. I reckon the sand and heat get old after a while. Is that what brings you to Velbridge?"

Caden chuckled. "Something like that."

He'd read over the transfer letter many times as he traveled, practically committing it to memory. There was no mention of his suspected crime or the reason he was transferred.

"You wanting to be a Runesman?"

"I am one, actually."

"Oh? Lord D'Lance has many, but he's always looking for more. Being favored by the High Prince comes at a steep cost, especially since he plays the part of a peacekeeper. All these lords who think that nobility is a pissing contest have to constantly be reminded of their proper place."

"It sounds like I'll see plenty of battle," Caden

said.

"Oh, I'll wager you'll see plenty more than you'd like. Word is spreading that some upstart is talking about starting a war." Angus shook his head. "Lord D'Lance will quell it, but when the High Prince finds out, there'll be hell to pay."

Despite the severity of what Angus was saying, Caden was excited. His plan initially had been to transfer to a Dominion where he would see more battle, so his luck couldn't have been better. Now he just needed to make a name for himself on the battlefield, and the riches would follow.

"How much training have you had?"

"A week or so," Caden replied sheepishly. "I'd planned on being fully trained before transferring, but it didn't work out that way."

As they talked, Angus led him across the courtyard and around the eastern side of the castle. Roughly a hundred feet away sat a large rectangular building. It was built of the same gray stone as the castle, but the decoration was lacking. They went inside, and Caden realized it was the barracks. As with everything else he'd seen so far, it put Lord Klodian's to shame. There were two levels, and there was enough room to house a few thousand soldiers.

"Is this where I'll be staying?" Caden asked.

"Yes. This is the Runesmen barracks. The barracks for soldiers without runes is on the opposite side of the castle."

"How many Runesmen does Lord D'Lance have?"

"I believe at last count it was upwards of five thousand."

Caden's eyes widened in surprise. "When you said he had many Runesmen, you weren't exaggerating."

"If there's anything you'll learn about the Dracan Dominion, it's that Lord D'Lance has the best of everything."

Five thousand Runesmen. Caden couldn't imagine how strong Lord D'Lance could be with that many men at his disposal. Was it even possible for someone to utilize the attributes of that many people? Perhaps his excitement had been premature. How would he make a name for himself as a soldier with so much competition?

"I assume your previous lord cut the rune he gave you?"

Caden's hand instinctively went to the back of his neck, rubbing the tattoo.

"No," he replied. "Should he have?"

Angus paused and turned to look at him. "Let me see it."

Caden obliged, turning around. Angus pulled the neckline of his shirt back and muttered something he didn't catch, then said, "A strength rune. Not many of those in our ranks lately."

"Why not?"

"As I said, Lord D'Lance pays a steep price for being the favorite. Runesmen get used a lot around here. Without proper rest and time to heal, burnout becomes a problem. Some can push through, but most can't."

"They get discharged?" Caden asked.

"No. They die."

Caden was glad that Angus couldn't see his face at that moment. Angus straightened his collar and continued further into the barracks. Caden rushed to catch up, and they ascended a stairway that led to the second level. The setup was similar to the first level, but there was a walled-off area with a door at the far end. Angus took him to the door and opened it, then motioned him inside and closed the door.

"Have a seat."

Caden did so, seating himself at one of the chairs in front of a large desk. Angus walked around to the other side and sat down, clasping his fingers together and leaning forward.

"I hope you'll forgive my ruse, but we have many soldiers that transfer here, and most of them don't have what it takes to serve Lord D'Lance."

"*You're* the captain," Caden said with a nervous laugh.

"Commander, actually. Commander Angus Morin. Do you have your letter of transfer?"

"Yes, sir." Caden set the parchment on the desk and slid it forward.

Angus picked it up and read over it, then set it atop a stack of papers.

"I'm good at reading people, Caden. In my position, I have to be. I can tell you're ambitious, else you wouldn't have requested to come here of all places."

Caden smiled, but he knew that he'd had nothing to do with where he'd been sent. He didn't think it would hurt to leave that information out.

"I like you," Angus continued. "Normally, I'd send you out with the next patrol to get your feet wet with something like settling a border dispute, but I've got something different in mind. I find it curious that your rune wasn't cut. It severs the magic between you and your lord, allowing a new rune to be added."

Caden assumed he knew where the conversation was going. Angus probably thought he was a spy. Why else would his rune be intact? Had Lord Klodian believed Eduard's suspicions and sent him to the Dracan Dominion, thinking that this was his true home? Caden swallowed hard and tried not to let his emotions show.

"There was a lot going on, so it's possible that Lord Klodian forgot."

"That's possible," Angus said. "I get the feeling you think this is a bad thing. Let me put your mind at ease now. It's fine."

"I was a little worried," Caden admitted.

"Don't be. Things couldn't be better for you."

Caden relaxed, the invisible weight on his shoulders washing away.

"In fact, I think Lord D'Lance is going to take a personal interest in you."

3

You.

The dragon's voice echoed within Mina's mind. She stood still, frozen in place. For some unfathomable reason, she'd envisioned this entire situation going differently. The dragon shifted his bulk and slithered around to fully face her, his hot breath washing over her like the heat from a fire.

Why do you stalk me? Do you seek death at the claws of a dragon?

While terror kept her physically rooted in place, Mina was able to push through the fear mentally. She could feel a plethora of emotions coming from the dragon, all of them swirling together. The one that stood out the most was curiosity. It smelled sweet, reminding Mina of strawberries, with subtle notes of honey and mint.

You can *speak,* Mina said, pushing the words through the scale.

All dragons can speak.

Can they? I've always heard that dragons were ... She paused, knowing that if she completed the sentence, the dragon would likely snap her in two.

That we are dull? I can assure you that we dragons are far from lacking intelligence. Tell me, girl. Why have you come?

Abruptly, the feeling of dread she felt

dissipated. Her muscles slackened, and she blinked. Her lips were chapped from the heat and the sand, and she ran her tongue across them, but it did little to help.

"Why can I hear you?"

The dragon tilted his head to the side, and his pupils became thin slits.

I believe the scale in your leg has something to do with that.

"Well, yes, but *why?*"

The dragon snorted. *How would I know?*

"The scale came from a dragon, and you are a dragon. I thought you would know."

I do not.

The two stared at one another in silence, and Mina considered how crazy it all was. She was talking to a dragon—a dragon!—and it felt normal, as though she were conversing with another person.

I hope that you did not come all this way to ask me a single question. I've eaten people for much less.

"I have many questions. Why were you afraid before? In the mesa when you tried to kill my mast—my lord?"

Dragons fear nothing, he replied heatedly. *You mistake mercy for fear.*

"Mercy? You and the other two dragons fled as if you'd seen a spirit."

I have spoken already. What else do you want to know?

"Can you remove the scale?" Mina asked.

The dragon stepped closer, snaking his head down until his eyes were level with her.

Let me see the scale.

Mina opened her mouth to protest, but the dragon glared at her. She reached down and unbuttoned her pants, then slid them down to reveal the scale. The dragon stared at it intently, then returned his gaze to her face.

It cannot be removed.

"Why not?"

It has fused into your flesh and become a part of you. To remove it would kill you.

"What of the curse? Can it be lifted?"

What curse do you speak of?

"This blasted thing allows me to feel the presence of dragons. And now I can hear you speaking through it. How do I get rid of the curse if I can't get rid of the scale?"

The dragon drew back and sat on its haunches, its tail flicking back and forth behind it. Mina pulled her pants back up.

You are the reason my brethren are being killed. A growl rumbled in the dragon's chest. *I had assumed the man killing us was using magic to find us, just as he uses it to become stronger and faster.*

Instead, it is you.

Mina didn't feel guilty. She helped Klodian because she believed that ultimately it would help her be free. Her face remained impassive as she stared up at the dragon. It towered over her, but oddly, she wasn't afraid.

I can feel your hatred. Why do you despise us so much?

"Why do you think?" Mina patted her leg. "This thing ruined my life. I've been a slave most of my life because of it." She could feel the anger welling up within her.

How is that our fault? Did one of my kind force the scale into your flesh?

"No. I fell into a nest and landed on it."

And you blame us for that?

The dragon was trying to get into her head. She refused to question herself on this. Dragons *were* to blame. They had caused all of her problems, whether this one wanted to accept that or not.

"The blame lies with one of you, and I won't rest until you're all dead."

The dragon moved with lightning quickness. His massive claw snatched her from where she stood and slammed her onto the ground, pinning her in place. Mina's heart pounded wildly in her chest, and the fear she'd felt before returned full force.

You are nothing to me, girl. You pose no threat. Your words are the howling of the wind against the mountain and nothing more. I could crush you with little effort.

"Then do it."

Mina couldn't believe the words had come from her mouth. She tensed, expecting the dragon to stomp down on her. The dragon only stared at her in silence. The scent of an unfamiliar emotion poured off the dragon, but she didn't know what it was. It smelled of a mix between lemon and clove.

You are not afraid to die?

"No."

Then you are not like the others of your race. The dragon leaned down and sniffed her. *What is your name?*

"Mina."

Mina, the dragon repeated it, and her name echoed over and over within her mind.

"What is your name?"

You will know my name once you earn my trust, girl. For now, you may call me Copper.

Copper. She didn't find the nickname very original, considering his color, but it was better than nothing. She squirmed under the force of his claw, but he didn't let her up.

In exchange for sparing your life, I demand that you stop leading your lord to my brethren.

"You didn't spare my life," Mina said. "And I told you I'm not afraid to die."

The scent of your fear says otherwise. And I could have flamed you and your horse long before you reached the summit of this mesa.

"You knew I was coming here?"

Yes.

"Why didn't you evade me like you've been doing?"

Your determination made me curious.

"Could you smell me? Or how did you know I was approaching?"

The power of your scale works both ways for a dragon wise enough to know how to sense it.

Mina had suspected that, but the idea that a dragon could sense her as she was able to sense them had made her uneasy, so she chose to ignore that possibility. Now that she knew the truth, it only added to her list of questions.

Now, give me your oath.

"Let me up first."

Copper lifted his claw and Mina rolled away and got to her feet. She looked up at the dragon, weighing her options. Lord Klodian had been too busy to go on his hunts, and if there really was a war brewing, she doubted he would have the free time for one anytime soon. And if there was no war, she could just lead him around aimlessly until he gave up.

"I will not lead him to any more dragons," Mina said. "For now."

For now?

"I have more questions. As long as you answer them, I will hold up my end of this bargain."

What makes you think you have any power over this agreement?

Mina smiled. "Because Lord Klodian has one of your eggs."

4

Caden stood in the shadows of an alley behind a busy tavern called *The Dirty Serpent.*

The sound of raised voices and laughter spilled out from the place, signs that the patrons were thoroughly enjoying themselves, including his target. Angus had given him the task of removing a threat to Lord D'Lance.

"I'm a soldier, not an assassin," Caden had argued.

"I know that I am asking much from you, but this man is dangerous. He doesn't know your face, so you'll be able to get close to him before he realizes what's happening. If you are successful, I'll take it as proof of your skill. It needs to be quick, but not public."

"Why doesn't Lord D'Lance deal with him directly?"

"Politics, my boy. They are as nuanced as the weaving of a tapestry. Lord D'Lance is a public figure. He can't just go around killing his enemies without backlash. Things like this must be done delicately."

Caden understood those things, which was the only reason he agreed to do the job. He would have preferred handling a border dispute or some other task, but it seemed like Angus trusted him. Since he was eliminating a dangerous foe, he was essentially protecting Lord D'Lance's life. He would make a name for himself yet.

A soft whistling sound echoed down the alley. That was Caden's sign. He unsheathed the dagger Angus had given him and crouched beside the door that led into the kitchen. Muffled voices were speaking on the other side. Caden gripped the hilt tightly, preparing himself. He didn't feel right about killing an unarmed man, but he pushed those feelings down deep inside. The door opened and a figure stepped out into the alley.

"Joeffrey?"

"Over here, sir," Caden whispered.

"What in the blazes are you doing in the dark?"

"It's urgent, sir. I need to show you something."

The figure glanced around the alley, then walked toward Caden. As soon as he was within range, Caden leaped forward and drove the dagger into the man's stomach. There was a pained grunt, but Caden's didn't feel any blood. The man staggered back, cursing, and stepped into the moonlight. He was wearing chainmail under his shirt.

Caden tackled the man, and the two of them crashed to the ground. His target was stronger than he looked, and he almost managed to get the dagger from his grasp. Caden ended up on top of the man and leaned forward, putting all of his weight into the movement. The dagger's blade sliced through the man's hand and drove into his neck. There was a gurgled cry, and then silence.

Death was no stranger to Caden, but he'd never murdered someone before. It left a foul taste in his mouth and made him feel dirty somehow. He got to his feet and waited, watching the blood pool around the man to ensure he was dead. Satisfied, he hurried down the other end of the alley and emerged onto the main street.

The roads weren't as packed as they had been during the day, but there were still people ambling along. Most of them were probably heading to and from the many taverns in Velbridge, and Caden did his best to keep his face hidden as he passed them. No one knew what he'd done, but the guilt he felt had a funny way of making him think they did. By the time he returned to the castle, he felt horrible.

Angus met him at the gates, and they walked wordlessly to the barracks. They went up to the second level and into Angus's office, and Caden collapsed into a chair. Not only was he feeling sick from his actions, but he was tired. He'd been in Velbridge for less than a day and he had blood on his hands. Figuratively, if not literally. He looked down to see if there was any blood visible and noticed his hands were shaking.

"I assume it's done, then?" Angus asked.

Caden nodded.

"Good. You've done the Dominion a great service. Lord D'Lance will be glad to know that there is one less enemy in our midst."

"Sir, I … I don't feel right about it. That wasn't battle. It was murder."

Angus sat on the edge of his desk and stared Caden straight in the eyes. He remained silent for a moment.

"As a soldier, you need to remove your feelings from the situation. You were given a task, and you completed it. With that said, I'd be worried if you didn't feel remorse. You took a life, which is no small thing. Yet you saved Lord D'Lance from a possible assassination. The man you killed has been here for weeks, waiting for an opportunity to catch us off guard. He was an agent of the lord I told you about, the one wanting to start a war. I wasn't exaggerating when I said you've done a great service."

Angus's words eased Caden's guilt a little, but they didn't make him feel any less dirty.

"Take one of the open beds and get some rest. Work through your feelings if you must, but be ready in the morning."

"Ready for what?" Caden asked.

"To meet with Lord D'Lance. He'll be glad to have a strength Runesman, but when I tell him what you've done for the Dominion, I expect there will be great things in store for you."

"Thank you, sir."

Caden rose from the chair and left the office. He'd left his bag with his belongings in an empty chest at the end of one of the beds, and he lifted the lid to see that his stuff was still there. Between his journey and his gruesome task, he felt soiled. He grabbed a fresh pair of clothes from his bag and changed, tossing the ones Eduard had given him into the bottom of the chest. He didn't plan on wearing them again.

Most of the beds on the second level were empty, but here and there, Caden spotted sleeping soldiers. He climbed onto the cot and stared at the ceiling. He'd murdered a man. That was disturbing enough, but the more troubling thing was that it hadn't been hard for him to do. He wanted to blame it on his willingness to prove himself, but he wasn't sure that was the source.

He was still angry about Thais, and it felt good to take that anger out on someone. Did that make him a bad person? He hoped not. He pleaded silently to any god that was listening to forgive him, then his thoughts turned to Mina. He hadn't gotten to speak to her after he'd kissed her, and he still feared that he may have upset her.

Perhaps deep down, he truly was a monster.

5

Lord Klodian had found the egg a few years previous.

It had been in one of the nests that Mina had led him to, and he took the egg back to the castle. She never knew why he decided to take it, but it never hatched. Eventually, everyone around the castle had lost interest in it.

Despite that, Lord Klodian had continued to keep it secured beneath the castle. Mina didn't know exactly where it was located, but she had a general idea. The only problem she could foresee was whether he still kept the room guarded.

Since Copper had begrudgingly agreed to help her find a way to remove the scale from her leg in exchange for the egg, she had to figure out a way to abscond with it. It wasn't likely that Klodian would realize it was missing until long after it was gone, and if Mina was free of the curse, she'd be long gone as well.

"My Lady," a servant greeted as he passed her in the hall.

She smiled and continued to her room, Vhan's sword propped against her shoulder. Mina supposed she looked like a fool with the weapon. It was much too heavy for her, and she doubted she could properly swing it even if she wanted to. Still, she felt powerful when she carried it, and in a way, she considered it a remembrance of Vhan. She still couldn't believe that the squire was dead.

Lord Klodian had returned to the mesa the next day with a large force of Runesmen and retrieved the boy's body, and Mina had stood with the crowd at his pyre as he burned. Vhan had been honored, but it seemed to her as though everyone had quickly forgotten about him.

She was so deep in her thoughts that she walked right past her room without realizing it. She stopped at the edge of an open doorway and was about to turn around when she heard voices talking lowly.

"He doesn't have enough men to spare," a man said. "Lord Klodian is already hard-pressed to keep his Dominion safe from wild animals. How does Lord D'Lance expect him to send an army to aid against the brewing war?"

"Has Lord D'Lance sent a formal request?" It was a woman.

Mina didn't recognize their voices, but she knew they were nobles. Otherwise, they wouldn't be in this hall.

"Not yet, but he's bound to any day now. I have a feeling Lord Klodian will deny the appeal."

"I'm certain he will. He's been consumed with hunting dragons of late, and war in a far-off Dominion has nothing to do with him. He will deny Lord D'Lance, and that will be our moment to strike."

Mina scrunched her face. Were they plotting

against Lord Klodian? She quietly stepped closer to the doorway and tried to get a glimpse of who the voices belonged to. Unfortunately, they weren't within eyesight.

"We mustn't make any moves until we receive word. Lord Klodian will be replaced, but it must be at the appropriate time."

"What of the spy? I don't trust her. She isn't loyal by choice. You didn't hear me say this, but I think he made a mistake in sending her. He should have entrusted the task to someone else."

The weight of the sword was taking its toll on her, and Mina lowered it from her shoulder, trying to rest the tip on the floor. It scraped against the stones, and she winced.

"What was that?" the man asked.

Mina heard footsteps. She fled to the next room and slipped inside, hoping nobody was within. The room was empty, and she gently closed the door. She pressed her ear to the wood and listened intently.

"I don't see anyone," the woman said. "Still, we should probably continue this later."

There was more said, but it was muffled and Mina couldn't make out the words. She ground her teeth in frustration and waited until she no longer heard anything. Pulling the door open, she glanced out and saw the hall was clear. She hurried to her own room and locked the door, then placed the sword back on the wall.

She had so many concerns. Who were those people? And why were they plotting against Lord Klodian? Judging by their conversation, they were pawns to someone else, someone more powerful. They'd also mentioned a spy. She considered going to Lord Klodian immediately, but aside from what she'd overheard, she had nothing else to provide.

Mina frowned. She would have to figure out who those people were. It would also be helpful if she could find the spy. Although her new position had brought some attention to her, she'd spent years being ignored. Like the servants, she'd been privy to many secrets simply because people overlooked her. She was certain she could use that to her advantage, but she couldn't steal the dragon egg *and* uncover a coup.

She was going to need help. If Caden were still here, she could ask him. He'd been her only friend, and now that he was gone, she was alone again. She could ask one of the servants to watch the comings and goings of the noble's hall, but she didn't know if she could trust any of them. It had quickly become apparent that they were jealous of her new position, and if one of them could find a reason to sabotage her, she knew they would take the opportunity.

Mina paced her room. There had to be someone she could enlist, but who? Her mind continued to draw a blank, so she turned her thoughts to the egg. If no guards were watching over it, she could easily sneak it out of the castle and deliver it to Copper. However, if there were eyes on it, she'd have to have a backup plan.

If only there was a guard she could trust to help her get inside and avoid any trouble. Her face lit up. She knew just who to turn to.

6

It took less than a full day for Caden to realize that the Dracan Dominion operated much differently than the Thophate. Aside from the assassination he'd performed the night previous, it was also evident in the way the Runesmen were organized. Since there were so many of them, they were divided into groups commanded by captains. The captains reported to Angus, who in turn reported to Lord D'Lance.

"Which company will I be assigned to?" Caden asked as he followed Angus through the castle.

"That depends on how your conversation with Lord D'Lance goes. If it goes as well as I think it will, you'll report directly to me."

"I'm afraid I don't understand."

"You will," Angus replied.

They arrived at a circular room that was lined with wooden benches. The room was packed with people that had bored expressions on their faces.

"This is the Coterie. Anyone who wants an audience with Lord D'Lance must come here and wait. If he has the time to hear their cases, they are summoned into the Cathedra."

Caden glanced around the room, counting at least fifty people. "Lord D'Lance is going to see all these people today?"

"No. Depending on his other priorities, he might accept five of them."

As Angus approached the large double doors that led into the Cathedra, the crowd of people parted to allow him access. Two guards dressed in ceremonial armor and armed with halberds bowed their heads and hurried to open the doors. A few of the waiting people groaned, and Angus snapped a glare at them.

"Apologies, milord," one man said. "I've been here for the last three days waiting. I was told I'd be next."

"My business with Lord D'Lance will be quick," Angus said. "It shouldn't impact your meeting."

"Thank you, milord."

Angus nodded at Caden, and they walked through the doors and into a much larger chamber, though this one was rectangular in shape. A plush purple rug at least thirty feet in length covered the floor, and guards were lined up along the walls. The room was lavishly decorated, and Caden felt as if he was walking in the court of the High Prince rather than a Dominion Lord.

Angus stopped at the edge of the rug and clasped his hands behind his back. Caden wasn't sure of the protocol, and so he mirrored Angus's posture. At the other end of the room, an enormous throne sat atop a raised platform. Caden squinted to see Lord D'Lance, but the lighting was dim and he was hidden within the shadows.

Standing at the base of the platform was a woman. She was petitioning Lord D'Lance to send soldiers to find her son.

"He's been missing for a week, and it isn't like him. I fear something may have happened to him near the abandoned temple," she said.

A man Caden hadn't noticed before leaned close to the throne as if listening, then stood straight and spoke with a loud voice.

"My Lord D'Lance has taken note of your concern, and he will be sure to have some Runesmen investigate your son's disappearance. Please go in peace."

The woman bowed low, then turned and made her way to the doors. Caden saw her face as she passed. She looked exhausted, and there were dark bags under her eyes. Once she had left the Cathedra and the doors were closed, the man beside the throne beckoned.

"My Lord D'Lance welcomes his faithful servant Commander Morin and his guest."

"Don't speak until Lord D'Lance acknowledges you," Angus whispered.

"Yes, sir."

Caden stepped onto the rug and was amazed at how soft it was beneath his feet. Even with his boots on, it felt as if he was walking on the clouds. At the end of the rug, Angus knelt on one knee and bowed his head. Caden did the same, and he watched from the corner of his eye for the commander to rise. He remained bowed for a long moment, then lifted his head.

"Rise," the man said.

Caden stood, glancing from Angus to the throne. Despite being only a few feet away from it, the shadows still hid Lord D'Lance from view.

"How goes the task of finding the dissenter?"

It was the herald again. He was of average height, bald, and without facial hair. Caden took note of his face, which was thin and clearly hadn't seen the sun much.

"He has been found and eliminated," Angus replied.

"Who is your guest?"

"This is Caden Davtyan, a Runesman from the Thophate Dominion."

Silence settled over the group, and a new voice spoke, one that made Caden's skin crawl.

"Leave us."

The herald bowed and hurried off without another word. Lord D'Lance stood and stepped into the light. He looked nothing like Caden had imagined. He was tall and thin, with long black hair that flowed down past his shoulders. He wore purple robes trimmed in gold, and his facial features reminded Caden of a hawk. Pointed, pronounced, powerful.

"This is the Runesman you told me about, is it not?"

"Yes, my Lord. I sent him to deal with Terlamin last night."

"And he was successful?"

"Yes. I verified that it was his body myself."

Lord D'Lance turned his icy gaze on Caden, and it seemed as if the man had the uncanny ability to see straight into his soul, slicing through the layers of his being like a hot knife through wax.

"My commander tells me that your former Dominion Lord did not cut your rune before you left. Is this true?"

"Yes, my Lord," Caden answered.

"Tell me, Caden, what do you aspire to be? What are your wants? Your needs?"

The look in Lord D'Lance's eyes made Caden uncomfortable. There was something about the man that set off warnings in his mind, but other than his demeanor, there was nothing visible that justified the discomfort.

"I want fame and fortune."

"A man after my own heart." He smiled. "I assume that is why you've come to my Dominion. My arm stretches farther than any other … aside from the High Prince, of course. How do you seek to find these things?"

"I'm a Runesman, my Lord. I am willing to fight to earn it. Literally."

"I see why you brought him to me, commander. He is ambitious beyond his reach. And loyal, it seems. Commander Angus gave you a task your first day here, and you completed it. I need a man of your strength and character. There are many enemies on the prowl, and I fear I do not have enough people that I can trust to aid me. Can I trust you?"

"With your life, my Lord."

"Perhaps one day you will earn that privilege," Lord D'Lance said. "How would you like to serve me directly, Caden? Doing so will earn you the fame and fortune you seek."

"It would be my honor."

Lord D'Lance looked back at Angus. "He doesn't know what he's getting himself into, does he?"

The two shared a knowing smile, and Caden began to ponder that very question.

"I'm sure you've heard that war is brewing on the horizon. Lord Culver in the Toren Dominion has been breathing threats against the High Prince. Not openly, of course, but his words have reached my ears. It is my duty to protect the High Prince from all enemies. I have men gathering the evidence I need to remove him from his seat of power, but until then, my attention is upon other things."

Caden wasn't sure where Lord D'Lance was going with all of his words, but he suspected that it would involve him somehow.

"How well did you get to know Lord Klodian?"

"Not very well, my Lord," Caden replied.

"A pity. I have reason to believe he's involved with Lord Culver's plot against the High Prince. If someone could give me information that swayed me in one direction or another, it would be most helpful."

"I know that he's obsessed with hunting dragons, but that's about all I learned before I was transferred."

"Dragons, you say? Intriguing. I, too, have an interest in dragons, but it does not involve killing them. Some people are just barbarians."

Lord D'Lance stared at Caden for a moment.

"I have a task for you. Commander Angus will give you the details, but there is another enemy that has come to my attention. If you can successfully handle this task, you will have my full and unwavering trust."

"Consider it done, my Lord."

Lord D'Lance smiled. "We shall see."

7

"You're insane," Thais said.

"That makes two of us."

Thais glared at her, but Mina didn't shrink away.

"You want me to help you steal something from Lord Klodian, and you don't see a problem with that? Your promotion must have gone to your head."

"It is a risk, I'm not denying that, but it's for the greater good."

"How so?"

Copper hadn't sworn Mina to secrecy, but she doubted anyone would believe her tale of talking dragons. People considered them nothing more than mindless animals, and she knew the world wasn't ready to accept the truth.

"I can't say. You'll just have to trust me."

"You seem to forget who you're talking to. I don't trust anyone."

Mina knew it was going to be difficult to convince Thais to help her, but she had to try. There were no other options.

"I don't need you to physically take the thing, I just need a diversion. If the guards can be lured away somehow, I'll do the stealing."

"Like I said, you're insane."

"What if I told you there's a spy here from another Dominion?"

Thais's eyes narrowed. "What spy?"

"I overheard two people talking about it," Mina replied. "I didn't see who they were, but they were talking about overthrowing Lord Klodian."

"Keep your voice down," Thais warned, glancing around the barracks. "Talk like that will get you strung up on the gallows, no matter who you are."

"Sorry," Mina said lowly. "I need help. Now that Caden is gone, I have no one else to ask. I can't do this on my own."

Thais frowned, but she leaned in close. "I won't have to go anywhere near this thing you're stealing, right?"

"No."

"I'll help you on one condition. I want to know who these people are that were talking about getting rid of Lord Klodian."

"I told you I don't know who they are," Mina said.

"Would you recognize their voices?"

"I think so."

"Then your task should be easy. Wander around the castle and listen for their voices. When you find out who they are, tell me. Once that's done, I'll help you with your theft."

Mina wanted to argue that they might run out of time, but she couldn't without explaining how. Copper had threatened to bring a host of dragons upon Klodian Keep, but when she agreed to steal it for them, it had satisfied his anger. She hadn't given the dragon a firm timeline, but she feared that if it took her too long, Copper would rescind his end of the bargain.

"Fine," Mina agreed.

She left the barracks, planning to go find Copper and tell him that she was working on getting the egg for him. She felt like she was being stretched too thin. Between stealing the egg and figuring out who the traitors were, she had a full plate. Still, the prize at the end of it all was worth it. She would finally be free of the scale and could make a new life somewhere else.

A gust of wind stirred up the dust of the courtyard, and Mina turned her gaze toward the gates. Dark clouds were on the horizon, and they flickered with lightning.

"Great," she muttered.

If she was quick enough, she should be able to reach Copper and get back to the castle before the storm struck. Mina hurried to the stable and found Aram laying fresh hay in the stalls.

"I need to take Tempest," she said. "Can you saddle her for me?"

"I'm afraid not," Aram said. "There's a storm

coming, and you don't want to be caught out there in it, believe me."

"It'll be quick," Mina protested. "I promise."

"I'm sorry, my Lady, but it's Lord Klodian's rule, given the recent disappearance of patrols. Unless you have written permission?"

She shook her head. "I don't."

"Then you'll have to wait until after the storm passes."

Mina stepped out of the stable and looked at the gates. She considered going on foot, but there was no way she would be able to reach the mesa before the storm hit, let alone get back safely. She returned to the castle, hoping that Copper didn't get impatient enough to bring an army of dragons.

Since Thais wouldn't help her until she found out who the traitors were, she decided to start with that task first. She'd overheard them in one of the rooms in the noble's hall, so it made sense to start there. Mina navigated her way through the maze of halls and reached her room. She paused at the door, listening for the sound of servants. If any of them were working in the hall, she didn't want them to see her sneaking around.

All was silent.

Mina moved along the hall, keeping her steps light. She went straight to the room she'd heard the two people conversing in. The door was closed. She turned the handle slowly and pushed the door open, peering inside. It appeared to be empty, so she stepped across the threshold and shut the door behind her.

The room was similar to her own chamber. An enormous bed covered by a sheer canopy was up against the wall. Side tables were on either side of it, and a long dresser than doubled as a desk rested opposite the bed. Mina walked to the dresser and began going through the drawers. They were full of expensive clothing, jewelry, and other useless trinkets.

Mina assumed that if this was their room, there should be something incriminating to be found. As she continued to search, however, she didn't find anything that gave her any clues. She knew it was possible that the two conspirators could simply have been using the room for their conversation, but she didn't think that was the case.

"Where would *I* hide something if I was a spy?" she asked aloud.

She spun in a circle, looking around the room. Nothing was out of the ordinary, but she knew there had to be something. The window rattled, startling her. She walked to it and looked out. The storm had already reached the castle. Even if she had taken the horse, she would have been caught in it. She silently thanked Aram for refusing her. With the disappearance of the patrols, people had begun to whisper that there was some sort of creature or spirit responsible.

Mina wasn't so sure of that, but she did find it curious that the patrols had vanished without a trace. Outside of the castle, the wind howled like a demon from the underworld. It was so loud that she didn't hear the door open.

"What are you doing in here?"

8

As Caden walked with Angus out of the throne room, he wondered if he was going to have to kill again. Captain Eduard's words echoed in his mind.

There's more to being a warrior than killing someone.

It was his duty to protect the Dominion Lord, true, but he felt more like an assassin than a soldier. Sneaking around and murdering people in the dark wasn't what he had in mind when he'd become a Runesman.

Yet if he wasn't willing to do it, someone else would. Someone else would gain the fame he sought for himself. Caden didn't like feeling dirty, but he supposed the path to what he desired would require him to get his hands bloody on occasion. Once they had left the Coterie behind, Angus filled him in.

"The enemy Lord D'Lance mentioned is extremely dangerous, but you won't be alone. We'll be transporting her to a place outside of the castle where she won't pose a threat to anyone."

"She, sir?"

"Yes. This enemy is a female."

Caden frowned. "We have to kill a woman, sir?"

"No, we won't be killing her. That's easier said than done, I'm afraid. We're just going to neutralize the threat."

Relief washed over him. He didn't know that he would have been able to carry out that task. Whether this woman was dangerous or not, he wasn't confident that his nerve wouldn't fail. Then he thought of Thais. He could harm her, but that's because it was personal. He didn't know this other woman.

"You'll be assisting Captain Burke and his Runesmen," Angus continued. "She'll be delivered to a makeshift prison and left there. If all goes well and you return alive, Lord D'Lance will be very pleased."

Caden's curiosity about the woman grew the more Angus talked about her. How could one person be so dangerous that it required an entire contingent of Runesmen to handle them?

"You seem distracted," Angus said.

"My apologies, sir. I'm trying to wrap my mind around the fact that one person can pose such a huge threat. I'm finding it difficult to believe."

"You'll learn why soon enough. Get yourself some food and go see Burke. He'll give you some new armor."

"What's wrong with my armor?" Caden asked.

"It's antiquated compared to what we have here. Keep it if you feel you must, but for this mission, you'll need to wear what Burke gives you."

"Yes, sir."

Angus left him, splitting off and turning down a different hall. Caden was glad that he could grab a meal before going back out on the road. His stomach felt empty, a reminder that he hadn't eaten dinner the night before. He got turned around while trying to get out of the castle and ended up roaming a corridor that seemed abandoned.

There were no tapestries adorning the walls, no rugs on the floor, and no guards. There were no people at all, which made the atmosphere eerily quiet. Caden had the feeling that something bad must have happened here. He was about to turn around when he heard something that caught his attention.

He stopped walking and listened. The sound was coming from somewhere further down the hall. Caden trod lightly, curiosity driving his steps. The closer he got, the more he was convinced that the sound was a muffled cry. He reached the door where the noise was coming from and pressed his ear against the wood.

It sounded like someone was in pain, but it was muffled as if they were gagged. Caden tried the handle. It was locked. Was someone being tortured? He supposed the room could be the dungeon. That would explain the lack of decorations and people, but if prisoners were being kept inside, there should at least be guards.

He tried the handle again, more forcefully this time, but it didn't budge. Whatever was going on behind the door didn't seem good. He felt that he needed to do something, but if he couldn't open the door, there wasn't much he could do.

"I need to tell Angus," Caden muttered.

Frowning, he backtracked his steps and eventually recognized his surroundings. He exited the castle and returned to the barracks. Angus wasn't in his office, so Caden made a mental note to ask him about the abandoned hall. Breakfast was being cooked on the first level, and the smell made his mouth water as he headed down the stairs.

A line of soldiers had formed near the kitchen, and Caden joined them. He overheard a few soldiers talking about the trouble brewing in Lord Culver's Dominion. Lord D'Lance had mentioned Lord Culver making threats against the High Prince, but if he wasn't making them openly, how did lowly soldiers know about it?

Caden received a tray packed with enough food for two meals. A glance at the other Runesmen around him revealed that they had been given the same treatment. Lord Klodian hadn't scrimped on food back in the Thophate, but Lord D'Lance took everything to the next level. Caden took his tray upstairs and sat on his bed, eating by himself and thinking about what the rest of the day held.

Once he was finished, he returned the tray to the kitchen. Since he didn't know what Captain Burke looked like, he picked someone at random and approached them.

"Excuse me, but I'm looking for Captain Burke. Can you point him out to me?"

"You'll know Captain Burke when you see him," the man replied with a grin. "He's probably the shortest one around here. He's got a bushy red beard, too."

"Are you talking about me behind my back?" The voice was deep.

Caden turned to the newcomer and had to hide his surprise. Captain Burke barely reached five feet in height. His shoulders were wide and his stocky frame was thick with corded muscle. He walked with a confident bearing and stalked over to them.

"No, sir," the soldier said. "I'd never speak about you behind your back, only above your head."

Captain Burke burst out in roaring laughter.

"You're hilarious, Halber. I think your joke just earned you kitchen duty tonight."

"I'm sorry, sir. I didn't mean to upset you."

"Oh, you didn't upset me. You just haven't learned your place here yet. It's my job to rectify that." Burke turned his gaze on Caden. "Were you in on the short jokes, as well?"

"No, sir. Commander Morin told me to find you. He said I'll be working with you to escort an enemy somewhere."

Burke grinned and stroked his beard, eyeing Caden up and down.

"I'm always glad to have help," he said. "Are you a Runesman?"

"Yes. I just transferred from the Thophate."

"Good! That means I don't have to train you. Judging by the looks of you, I'm guessing you have a strength rune?"

Caden nodded, impressed.

"Even better," Burke said. "We've lost a lot of strength Runesmen recently, so I'm glad to have you. You'll need different armor if you expect to come along, though. What you're wearing isn't going to hold up if things go south."

"What do you mean?" Caden asked.

"Did the commander tell you what we're escorting?"

"He told me we were escorting a woman. A dangerous one."

"Aye, but dangerous isn't the half of it. She's a wily one, and she don't take kindly to our kind."

Caden's face scrunched with his confusion. "I don't understand."

Captain Burke shook his head. "The commander didn't tell you, I take it?"

"Tell me what?"

"The prisoner is a dragon."

9

Mina whirled around, her heart dropping into her stomach, but relief washed over her when she saw it was Kera.

"I was looking for … them," Mina said.

"Who?"

"The lord and lady who reside here."

Kera folded her arms and stared at Mina. "What for?"

"That's not your concern," Mina replied.

"Spoken like one of the nobles. If you were really looking for them, you'd know they are with Lord Klodian right now. So, do you want to tell me what you are doing in here, or should I let Lord Klodian know you're riffling through his court member's personal effects?"

Mina decided to bluff.

"Lord Klodian already knows what I'm doing. He sent me here."

Kera's suspicious demeanor faltered. "He did?"

Mina nodded.

"Why didn't you just say that?"

"I was told to keep quiet about it. Court politics."

Kera rolled her eyes and dropped her hands to

her sides. "It's always something around here. One would think that being out here so far from the bigger Dominions that all that political nonsense wouldn't be an issue."

"It's worse than you know," Mina said. "But you didn't hear that from me."

"I'm sorry that you have to be involved in their games now. Freedom isn't really freedom, is it?"

Mina shrugged. "Most of my life has been this way, so it's not much of a change for me. I don't think I need to mention that you didn't see me in here and we never had this conversation."

"Of course not, my Lady. I'll just leave you to it, then."

"I do have a question. Whose room is this?" Mina's face flushed and she knew she was pressing the boundaries. "I wasn't told which room specifically to check, so I may not even be in the right place."

"I'm not surprised that no one gave you any sort of direction. The nobles like to assume we know everything even though they keep us in the dark. This is Lord and Lady Burgess's chamber."

"Then I am in the right room." Mina smiled, but inside she was a nervous mess.

"Anything else?"

"No, thank you."

Kera offered a nod and left the room. Mina rubbed her hands over her face, sighing in relief.

That had almost gone disastrously wrong. She continued searching the room, but there was nothing she could find that proved the two she'd heard talking were planning to overthrow Lord Klodian. She suspected they were working for someone, which meant there had to be a letter or something incriminating. Mina checked the same drawers again but turned up nothing.

Despite that, she had learned who they were. And since she had a name, that meant Thais would help her with the egg. The wind rattled the windows again, interrupting her thoughts, and Mina knew she would have to wait for the storm to pass to speak with Thais. She made sure to put everything back the way she'd found it and hurried to her own chambers, flopping onto her bed.

The day was still young, so Mina decided that once the storm was gone, she would speak with Thais and then ride out to let Copper know of her progress. She hoped that if she kept him apprised of things, he would keep his word. Then again, she didn't know that the dragon would honor what he said at all. He was a dragon, and she had a lot of trouble trusting him, but she didn't have much choice. He was her best chance of removing the scale from her leg, so she *had* to trust him.

That was the last thing she remembered before she awoke. Mina sat up and looked to the window. The storm was gone, and the sun shone brightly through the glass. She found it odd that she'd fallen asleep because she hadn't even been tired, but perhaps the stress of everything had taken its toll on her.

Mina slid off the bed and left her room, leaving Vhan's sword behind. She went to the barracks and found Thais and several other Runesmen sweeping dirt from the floor. Thais looked at her quizzically.

"I found out who those people are," Mina said.

"That was quick," Thais replied.

"Well, it was pure luck. I went snooping around in their room and one of the servants walked in on me. Anyway, she told me that they are Lord and Lady Burgess."

"Burgess?" Thais frowned. "I've never heard that name before."

"That makes sense. Considering what they are plotting, I doubt they would use their real names. Burgess is probably a fake surname."

"If that's true, then we're still at the beginning. Find out more about them."

"No," Mina said. "You told me to get you a name. I did that. Now it's your turn to help me. Besides, I didn't find anything in their room that seemed suspicious."

"Did you look for false drawers or hidden compartments?"

"No, why would I?"

"These people are spies," Thais replied. "They aren't going to leave things out in the open."

"How would I know that? I don't unravel

nefarious plots every day. In case you forgot, the most I've done until recently is clean things and lead Lord Klodian to dragons. You said you would help me, so unless you're going back on what you said, I need you to meet me tonight."

"*Tonight?*" Thais asked incredulously.

"Time is slipping away, and the danger grows with every hour that passes."

Thais looked around the barracks. "Fine. Where should I meet you?"

"Outside around midnight. The servants will be asleep by then, and I can sneak you into the castle without anyone noticing."

"Do you have a plan?"

"Yes. You'll cause a distraction, and I'll steal the e—item," Mina said, correcting herself at the last moment.

"How is that a plan? What kind of distraction am I creating?"

Mina shrugged. "Figure it out. I'm doing all the risky work."

"I don't like your attitude. I've got half a mind to wash my hands of all this."

"It's your duty to protect Lord Klodian and the Dominion. If you don't help me, you'll be shirking that duty."

"If we're in as much danger as you say, why don't you tell Lord Klodian? Wouldn't that simplify things?"

Mina wanted to tell Thais everything, but she didn't trust the woman. Not yet, anyway. Once this was all over with, maybe she would let her guard down a little.

"Lord Klodian doesn't need to be involved unless we fail. And by then, it'll be too late anyway."

"Do you know how to answer a question without being cryptic?" Thais asked.

"Yes, but as I said before, I can't tell you anything. If we manage to pull this off, then I'll reveal everything. Until then, you just need to do as I ask."

Thais chuckled. "You're an odd one, you know that? I'm still going to help you, but only because I'm curious. I don't believe we're in any danger, but if that's what drives you, so be it. Now get out of here before I get in trouble for not cleaning. I'll see you tonight."

Mina left the barracks and headed for the stable. It was time to go see Copper.

10

"A dragon?"

Caden didn't think he heard the captain correctly.

"Aye, a dragon. You ever seen one up close?"

"No, thank the gods. My previous lord liked to hunt them for fun, but I'd rather avoid them."

"You can stay behind if you want," Burke said. "But I wouldn't suggest it."

Caden knew that if he didn't go, his chance of earning Lord D'Lance's trust would be gone. He was afraid of dragons, but who wasn't? Burke didn't seem to be. Caden knew he would have to push through the fear, but he wasn't sure how.

"I'm going," he said.

"Good. First things first. We need to get you some armor."

"That's what Commander Morin told me."

"You'd be dead within seconds if a dragon flamed you, but we've got something that'll stand up to dragon fire. Come on, we'll get you fitted."

Caden followed Burke through the barracks, ending up in front of a steel door with several locks. Burke pulled a small ring of keys from his belt and methodically unlocked each one, but he didn't go in any specific order.

"This is the armory," Burke said. "Only those with the rank of captain or higher can get in, so if you need anything, you come to me."

Burke pushed the door open, motioning for Caden to go first. Caden stepped through the doorway and immediately noticed the large rectangular window that filled the space with plenty of natural light. A dozen or more racks of finely crafted swords were lined in orderly rows, and shelving units held breastplates, helms, and boots. One entire wall was covered with chainmail shirts that hung on hooks. Caden stared at them longingly.

"Those don't offer much protection against dragons," Burke grunted. "You'll be wearing full plate armor."

"I've never worn plate armor," Caden admitted. "Is it heavy?"

"Yes. It's also hard to maneuver in, but you won't have to worry about that. The dragon won't be walking around freely. The armor is just in case she escapes."

Caden didn't find much comfort in the man's words. His job as a soldier was to fight humans, not dragons. If the dragon escaped, he doubted any of them would live to tell the tale.

"What's so special about the armor?" Caden asked.

Burke grinned. "It's one of a kind. It'll protect you from dragon fire so long as you're wearing it properly."

"How? Doesn't dragon fire melt metal?"

"Aye, but this metal is different. It withstands high heat, acting as a buffer between you and the fire. A dragon could stand directly in front of you and blast away with its fiery breath, and you'll only feel a little warmth."

Caden stared at the armor dubiously until he remembered a conversation with Thais. She'd proposed a wild theory about someone using metal from some sort of creature that lived in volcanos. Was it possible that Lord D'Lance had actually pulled it off?

"You've seen it work?" Caden asked.

"I've got first-hand experience," Burke replied. "Find a breastplate that fits you snugly. You don't want any gaps at all."

Caden stepped over to the tall shelf and grabbed one that he thought would fit him, but when he slid it over his head, it was too big. He struggled for a moment to remove it, then set it back on the shelf and selected another. It fit perfectly.

"We've got a few helm styles. Pick the one you like best and grab a pair of boots."

"What about my arms and legs?" Caden asked.

"There are a few different bits that will piece together. Trust me, once you're fully suited up, there won't be an inch of you visible. Our blacksmiths have removed every possible flaw from the design."

"Sounds like the perfect armor."

"Lord D'Lance wouldn't accept anything less," Burke said. "We lose enough Runesmen as it is, so he spares no expense when it comes to protecting his soldiers."

"I appreciate that," Caden replied.

Burke turned and whistled, then waved someone over. Another man joined them in the armory.

"This is Kennet. He'll help you get the rest of the armor on because it's nigh impossible to do it on your own. Once you're done, meet me in the courtyard. We're leaving as soon as you're ready."

"Where are we going?" Caden asked.

"To escort the prisoner. Lock the doors when you're done," Burke said to Kennet, then marched off.

"I'm Caden. Thanks for helping me."

"It's no problem at all. Captain Burke isn't messing around when he says it's impossible to put this armor on alone."

"Are you a captain as well? He said only captains and above have access to the armory."

"I'm in training, so it's not official yet, but I do everything a captain does. I'll be taking over Captain Tayfur's position once Commander Morin signs off on me."

"Is Captain Tayfur retiring?" Caden asked.

"No. He was killed last week."

"Oh, gods. I'm sorry."

"Don't be," Kennet said. "He fell in battle during a border skirmish with Lord Culver's men. Culver's been slowly encroaching on Lord Veisi's Dominion for years, but it's become more aggressive recently. The commander has been sending a steady stream of Runesmen to Veisi's Dominion to deter any further action from Culver, but it hasn't seemed to make an impact."

"Sounds like a war is brewing."

"I don't know about that, but Lord D'Lance will have to do something before the High Prince learns about what's transpiring. The last thing anyone wants is for the High Prince to march his armies across Dominion lines. He'll let them ravage everything just to show his strength."

The more Caden learned about the politics of the Dominions, the less he wanted to know. He wanted wealth and fame, but he didn't want to be involved in the political sphere of things. That would only complicate his life, and he preferred things to be simple. His mind roamed as Kennet began strapping on pieces of armor to his arms.

By the time Kennet had finished, Caden felt as if his weight had doubled. The armor was considerably heavy, and even his boots had heft to them. Walking became so difficult it was a chore.

"Gods, how does anyone fight in this stuff? I can barely move."

"It's more for protection against dragon fire,"

Kennet said. "For battle, you'll probably wear chainmail. Since you're going with Captain Burke, you shouldn't have much to worry about. He's a competent man. It's pretty much assumed he's in line to become commander once Angus retires."

"Or dies?" Caden asked. It seemed to him lots of people died in this Dominion.

"I don't think Angus can be killed," Kennet said with a laugh. "That man has lived longer than most and seen more battle than anyone I know. Death herself will have to personally take him from this world. Let me tighten the strap on this vambrace, then you're all set."

Caden felt pressure around his left arm as Kennet pulled on the strap. Between the weight and the tightness of everything, he felt like he was being constricted to death.

"My suggestion is to leave the helm off until you get outside the walls. It traps in all your body heat, so I try to delay it as long as possible."

"Thanks," Caden said, gripping the helm with his right hand.

"You better hurry. Captain Burke isn't known for his patience."

Caden left the armory and exited the barracks, walking as quickly as he could manage. Halfway to where Captain Burke was waiting, he realized he'd forgotten to bring his sword. He dared not turn back and keep the captain waiting, so he continued around to the front of the castle.

"I forgot to grab my sword," Caden said as he approached Burke. "Do you want me to go back and get it?"

"No, we're already running behind schedule. I doubt we'll encounter any trouble. We're just taking this blasted creature to a new location and leaving her there to rot. The cage should hold her, but just in case, you may want to keep a wide berth of it."

Caden looked to where Burke indicated and swallowed hard. The cage was enormous, standing ten feet in height and at least twice that in length, not including the wheeled platform it was built upon.

"You ready for this?"

"As ready as I'll ever be," Caden answered.

"Good answer. Let's move out!"

11

Mina rode Tempest out into the desert, marveling at how the landscape had been changed by the storm. Typically, the dunes had flowing lines that made it seem as if they were rippling, but the wind had laid the sand down smooth and flat. She silently thanked Avera that Aram hadn't allowed her to leave earlier. The storm had struck quicker than she'd expected.

The scale in her leg alerted her to Copper's presence. He was on the same mesa that he'd been on the other day where she'd finally encountered him. Mina was dreading the climb to the top and was surprised when the dragon's voice resonated inside her mind.

Come to the base and I will bring you up.

How will you do that?

With my mighty wings. You humans are not very intelligent, are you?

We're smart enough to kill your kind, Mina fired back.

Copper's indignant snort gave her a bit of satisfaction. So, dragons had feelings and emotions about hurtful words just as humans did. That was interesting. She reigned the horse to a stop when she reached the mesa's looming walls.

Leave your horse and walk one hundred paces

from it.

Why? Mina grew suspicious, wondering if the dragon intended on killing her.

Although, if you prefer, I can frighten your mount away, but then you'd have to walk back to your castle.

Mina hadn't considered that. She dismounted and patted the horse on its neck. Tempest nudged her, and she fished an apple from the saddlebag and offered it to the animal. It took a bite and chomped loudly, then finished off what remained.

"Did you even taste that?" Mina asked, shaking her head. "Stay here and wait for me. I'll be back shortly."

She counted her steps as she walked away from the horse, following the mesa wall. When she reached one hundred exactly, she stopped and looked up. A shadow fell over her as Copper leaped off the top of the mesa, his wings outstretched. He spiraled around in circles, descending slowly. Despite her hatred for dragons, Mina found herself admiring the majestic beauty of Copper.

Sand billowed into the air in small clouds as the massive dragon's wings flapped to stop his descent. He landed a few feet away and Mina stared in silence.

Are you going to gawk all day?

Sorry.

Mina tentatively walked toward Copper, but she

didn't feel terrified of him.

The other day, I was frozen with fear, but I don't feel afraid now.

That's because I'm not projecting my pheromones.

What do you mean?

The dragon watched her intently as she approached. His slitted pupils remained fixed on her, unblinking.

We dragons can project a chemical into the air that lets other dragons know we're present. The fear you experience is a side effect. I think it's because humans don't know how to handle the pheromone.

Mina stopped in front of Copper, her eyes roaming over his scales. Here and there she spotted imperfections, knicks and scratches mostly, but a few scales were damaged and missing pieces entirely. His underbelly was the same color as the rest of his scales, and his claws were enormous. Talons as sharp as swords dug into the ground.

Why do you look at me so? Copper asked.

I've never seen a dragon up close before, Mina replied.

You saw me up close not long ago.

That was different.

She realized for the first time that the scale embedded in her leg didn't pain her. In the past, she'd have flaring pain that would cripple her anytime she got close to a dragon. Yet now, standing directly in front of one, she didn't feel that pain at all. And it had been the same the other two times she encountered him.

Are you ready?

Mina swallowed hard and nodded. *Should I climb on your back?*

Copper made a chortling sound that reminded her of laughter, and the scent of roses filled her nostrils. There were many things that she didn't understand about dragons, and she wondered how many of their secrets Copper would divulge to her.

Absolutely not. I'm going to grab you with my claws. Stretch your arms out. And don't squirm, else your flesh will slice off.

The dragon flapped his wings and rose into the air, then moved forward and extended his claws toward her. Before she could rethink her decision, Copper's front claws wrapped around her arms and he lifted her off the ground.

Mina clenched her jaw, fighting her instinct to scream. She watched the ground fade below her as the dragon rose higher and higher, the wind from his wings whipping at her hair and clothing. The top of the mesa became visible, and he set her down, then flew higher into the sky before streaking back down. He spread out his wings at the last moment, his upper body jerking upward while his rear legs touched the ground. She could hardly believe that a dragon could be so agile.

Can all dragons fly?

Yes. Can all humans walk?

Yes, Mina replied. *Well, most can.*

Most?

Some of us are born broken and cannot do certain things.

The same is true of dragons, Copper said. *But if a dragon cannot fly, it will not live long.*

Why not?

If the mother does not kill a hatchling before it leaves the nest, it will be prey for many creatures until it grows larger. Flying gives us the advantage of avoiding predators, and therefore killing a flightless dragon is a mercy.

What kind of animal hunts dragons?

Besides humans? Many things when we are small. Sand wyrms, mostly.

Mina's curiosity was piqued. *What's a sand wyrm?*

You have never seen one?

I don't think so.

You would know if you had. They do not come close to the places humans inhabit. They are found out here among the mesas sometimes. The further into the desert you travel, the more likely you will encounter them.

Mina didn't plan on going deep into the desert,

so she hoped she had nothing to worry about. Copper tilted his head to the side.

How goes the hunt for the egg?

That's why I came out here, Mina said. *I am going to try to take it tonight. I'll have help, so I should be able to deliver it to you tomorrow.*

That is good news. I hope that the egg is not damaged.

How long does it take for one to hatch? Lord Klodian has had the egg for a long time, but the egg remains unchanged.

Copper made a humming sound, and Mina smelled the faint hint of lavender. She didn't know why she smelled the aromas, but she had her suspicions that it had something to do with dragons.

Dragons can wait for years to hatch. The circumstances must be right, and the dragon will know whether it is safe to come out of its shell.

How many dragons are there?

Too many to count, Copper replied.

Do you get along with the other colors of dragons?

Many of them, yes.

How many colors are there?

Ten.

I've only seen five.

The metallic colors, I assume? We prefer the

solitude of the sand and heat. Our brethren, those whose colors are chromatic, do not.

Mina remembered the black dragon she'd seen on her trip with Lord Klodian when he'd taken her to test the scale's ability to sense magic.

Actually, I've seen six colors. One was black, but I saw him in the desert.

Truly? Copper's nostrils flared and his tail swished behind him. *I have not seen one of our brethren in many years.*

Why not? Mina asked.

They are the ones we do not get along with.

Care to explain?

It is a long story.

I've got some time.

Copper eyed her in silence for a moment.

Very well. The tale begins a thousand years ago ...

12

It was late in the evening when Captain Burke called a halt.

Caden pulled his helm off and breathed in deeply of the cool air. His entire body was drenched in sweat, and he couldn't wait to take the heavy armor off. Including himself, there were just over two dozen Runesmen. The massive wheeled cage that carried the dragon was pulled by ten Clydesdales, giant beasts that made normal horses seem minuscule in comparison.

The cage was really a boxcar, crafted of the same metal as their armor. There was a single door on one end that was reinforced with steel and covered with padlocks. Caden didn't know a lot about dragons, but he had the feeling that if the creature really wanted to get free, the meager defenses of the boxcar wouldn't be able to contain it.

"Gather round!" Burke shouted.

Everyone crowded in around the captain, forming a chaotic circle.

"We'll set up camp here. There's a hill not much further ahead where we'll be leaving her, but we'll need daylight, so we don't get the cage stuck on anything. I want two men on watch at each corner of the camp. If anyone on watch is caught sleeping, you'll answer to Commander Morin. Any questions?"

No one spoke.

"Good. Sabir and Lorn, you've got the east corner. Erik and Quinn, west corner. Dirk and Finnis, south corner. Asa and Boris, you're on the north corner. After two hours, wake someone to replace you. It should be a quiet night, but if you see anything, alert the camp. The dragon has been sedated and should be knocked out until after we're long gone, but keep away from the cage regardless."

The soldiers who had not been called for watch began retrieving bedrolls from the wagon that had followed behind the boxcar. None of them removed their armor, though, and they laid down with only their helms removed. Caden grabbed a bedroll for himself and looked for a place to rest. Most of his fellow soldiers had scattered out, but a few had grouped together.

He picked a spot near the wagon and rolled the bedroll out, but it did little to provide any comfort. The breastplate jabbed into his lower back, causing lances of pain to shoot through him with even the smallest movement. He forced himself into a sitting position and glanced around.

The camp was at the edge of a wooden area, and the landscape was mostly flat. Caden got up and carried his bedroll over to the tree line and placed the bedroll against one of the trees, then sat down and leaned back against it. While it still wasn't comfortable, it was better than lying flat on the ground.

His body ached from exhaustion, but he had difficulty falling asleep. The night sky above reminded him of the last time he'd seen Mina, and his thoughts grew dark. He'd spent a night in the dungeon and been forced to another Dominion because of Thais's actions. He had believed that she had feelings for him, but perhaps that was how she'd deceived him into letting his guard down. Eventually, his eyes grew heavy and he dozed off.

A scream startled him into wakefulness.

He clambered to his feet confusedly, rubbing his bleary eyes. It was still dark. The clash of steel echoed across the camp, and Caden realized they were under attack. He put his helm on and ran to the wagon, ducking behind it when he spotted two people outfitted in black armor. Emblazoned on their pauldrons was a clawed paw print surrounded by a blazing sun.

"Fall back!" It was Captain Burke. "To me, Runesmen! To me!"

Caden peered around the wagon and saw the captain was at the front of the boxcar. A handful of Runesmen was already with him, but everyone else was engaged with their attackers. He rushed to where Burke was and struggled to stop his momentum.

"What's going on?" he asked.

"Isn't it obvious? We're under attack."

"Yes, but by who? And why?"

"They're wearing the crest of Lord Culver,"

Burke answered. "The fool has gone too far this time. Lord D'Lance will have his head."

"Only if he finds out," Caden replied.

"What's that supposed to mean?"

Caden pointed ahead, and Burke turned his gaze to the direction he was pointing. A host of men in black armor bearing the same red crest of Lord Culver came rushing down the hill.

"Here," Burke said, handing a sword to Caden. "I trust you know how to use one?"

"I do."

"Good. If they release the dragon, we're dead for certain. We need to keep them from letting her out."

Caden gripped the hilt tightly and nodded. Despite the gravity of the situation, he couldn't help but consider how this would elevate him even further with Lord D'Lance should he survive. Excitement and fear flooded his senses in a confusing mix, just as it always did before a battle.

He lowered the sword and waited until one of the approaching men was close enough, then he stepped forward and swung his sword in an upward sweeping motion. The blade screeched against his opponent's breastplate and hit his helm, bouncing off and sending powerful reverberations through Caden's arm.

"We're outnumbered, but we won't go down without a fight!" Burke screamed.

The words bolstered Caden's spirit, and he pushed ahead, latching onto his opponent's arm and wheeling him around. He kicked the man in the chest, knocking him backward into the door of the boxcar. The force made the padlocks knock repeatedly against the metal frame, and Caden likened the sound to the clash of arms.

He spun back to face another enemy and saw one of his fellows get cut down. The man wasn't wearing his helm, and his head split open as a dark armored figure struck him from the side. Caden couldn't believe how many enemies there were. It seemed as if their ranks swarmed endlessly down the hill, decimating Burke's entire company of Runesmen.

"Things aren't looking too good!" He yelled at Burke.

The captain didn't reply, he just kept fighting, cleaving through the horde of shadowy men. Something bright flared ahead, illuminating the darkness. Caden turned his attention to the light and his eyes widened. The silhouette of a robed man was at the top of the hill, and a ball of flame swirled in front of him. The figure flicked his wrist and the flames soared down the hill, striking the wagon next to the cage.

"Forbidden magic," he whispered.

If things had looked bleak moments ago, they were doubly so now. Caden had never run from a fight before, but he'd only been in a few insignificant battles. If he stayed and fought, he was as good as dead. He backed up a few steps, every instinct telling him to turn and flee. But he didn't. For some unfathomable reason, he just stood there watching. Burke was struck down, and the remaining Runesmen fell quickly after him.

Run! He screamed within his mind, but his legs wouldn't obey him.

Caden watched the enemies turn from the corpses of his fellows and trudge back up the hill. They disregarded him as if he weren't even there, as though his presence was so insignificant, they didn't need to worry about him. The truth quickly became apparent, though, as the robed figure crafted another ball of flame and sent it hurtling through the air.

Caden's legs finally moved, and he stepped back and was about to turn around when the fiery globe struck the boxcar's door. There was a loud explosion and something hard and heavy struck the back of his head. He crumpled to the ground and fell into an ocean of darkness.

13

Mina sat on the ground with her legs crossed, staring up at Copper as he related the events of the past. His words swirled around her, creating images within her mind as if she had been there herself.

In those days, the relationship between humans and dragons was much different than it is today. We were allies, friends even. Dragon and man were bonded closely, sharing their minds.

Truly? Mina asked.

Indeed.

I've never heard that before. Until I met you, I always thought dragons were mindless animals.

There's a good reason for that.

Which is?

Copper growled, a rumbling sound that resonated from deep in his chest. Mina felt the ground tremble beneath her.

There are some things better left forgotten, he said. *And yet, there is a reason we met that day inside the mesa.*

What do you mean?

I am hesitant to reveal too much, but I feel that I must tell you things that you may not be ready to hear.

Mina's face creased. *If you think that I am weak, I'm not. I can handle anything you have to say.*

I do not think you are weak. If I did, I would not have let you find me. You'd still be wandering in the desert. No, girl, you are strong. Stronger than you know.

Mina caught the scent of lemon and clove.

Then tell me.

What you are about to learn must be kept a secret. You cannot share it with anyone. Give me your oath.

I promise I will keep the knowledge to myself, Mina said.

Good. Long ago, when our two kinds were friendly, division arose when a king among the humans named Maël decided to invade other lands. He tried to use us in his plot. The elders among the dragons refused, and a feud began.

Mina knew from her experience around Lord Klodian and the other nobles that they were always vying for supremacy over one another. It was almost as though it was human nature to want more for the sake of having it.

Did dragons and humans go to war?

Almost, Copper replied. *My kind was able to avert such a catastrophe.*

How?

We used magic.

Dragons can use magic?

Yes. We were formed of magic at the beginning of time, and so we can use it. The greatest and strongest of every color gathered and sacrificed themselves to power a spell so potent, that it is still in place today.

What was the spell?

I do not know the name of it, but it caused all of humankind to forget that dragons were allies. That was all it was supposed to do, but it also caused humans to forget that we were intelligent creatures.

What about me? Mina asked. *How is it that I haven't forgotten that you can speak?*

Once a human learns the truth, the spell no longer has sway over them.

Mina considered Copper's tale. She found it difficult to believe that dragons and humans were once friends. The unintended effect of the spell did answer a lot of questions, but it also left many more.

You are confused about something. What is it?

I don't understand why the dragons wanted us to forget about our alliance.

We didn't want to be used as weapons. We are much more than that.

You say 'we.'

Yes.

Why?

There was a pause, and Copper exhaled a long

breath through his nostrils.

I was there when it happened.

Mina's eyes widened. *How is that possible? That would make you ...*

Over a thousand years old.

I was going to say ancient.

Mina giggled, but Copper growled in annoyance.

I have lived a long life and seen many things, but I have never seen a human with a dragon scale in their flesh. I have thought long and hard about how it might be removed, but I fear I have not come up with an answer. Perhaps my brethren will find the solution.

Were you friends with any humans back then?

I was. One of my closest friends was a human.

What happened to him?

He died fighting against tyranny. When Maël began his invasion, he slaughtered innocent people. Those dragons and humans that were bonded fought against him. That was what led to the division between dragon colors as well. The chromatic dragons sided with Maël, claiming that he was just in expanding our kingdom.

Copper snorted.

There is no justice in murder, only darkness and evil. After the spell was cast, the chromatic dragons ceased to speak with us and disappeared. The rest of my brethren and I came to the desert to try and forget the past. Until Lord Klodian began hunting us down, we had found peace and solitude.

Mina didn't know what to say, so she remained quiet. Dragons and humans had once been friends. The thought still boggled her mind. She had despised dragons for most of her life. The idea that one could be her friend seemed so … foreign. Blasphemous, even.

You were bonded to your human friend, weren't you?

Yes. We shared our thoughts and desires with one another. We were a team with no rivals. We fought together until the day he fell.

What was his name?

Lucius. Copper blinked, and Mina swore she saw his eyes water. *It has been many years since I have spoken his name.*

I'm sorry, Mina said.

The emotion behind Copper's words was so strong, it was as if it were a palpable thing that she could touch. She didn't know why she apologized to the dragon. Perhaps it was the feeling of sadness he instilled in her. Or perhaps it was the feeling of losing someone close that resonated with her. She'd lost her parents, her friends, and her entire life when she'd fallen into that dragon's nest years ago.

Dusk is approaching. You should go. The desert is not a safe place during the night.

Your concern is touching, but I can take care of myself.

That remains to be seen, but I don't doubt your confidence. I must meet with my brethren regardless, so I cannot stay with you.

It's fine. I need to get back to the castle so that I can try and get the egg. With any luck, I'll have it for you tomorrow.

Copper extended his wings and stretched.

I hope you are successful, but if you are not, you are welcome to return empty-handed. I promise not to flame you into ash.

I appreciate that, Mina replied with a smirk.

Come, I will take you to the bottom of the mesa.

Just try not to rip my arms out of their sockets, will you?

I make no guarantees.

Mina stood and brushed the back of her pants off, then lifted her arms. Copper flapped his wings, ascending into the air a few feet above her. His claws encircled her arms and he carried her off the mesa. Mina's stomach dropped, but she found the quick flight exhilarating. Once she was safely on the ground again, she pulled her hair from her face and looked up at the dragon.

Good luck, Copper said.

Thank you. I'll need every bit, I think.

They sat in silence until Mina felt it was

awkward. She cleared her throat.

I'll see you tomorrow, then.

Farewell, Mina.

Copper launched himself into the sky, gaining altitude before turning to the south and disappearing over the top of the mesa. Mina returned to Tempest. The horse was stomping the ground impatiently.

"I'm sorry," she said. "I didn't intend to take so long. Here." She reached into the bag on the saddle and pulled out an apple and offered it to the animal. Tempest nickered softly and ate it, licking her hand in the process.

"Yuck." She wiped her hand on her pant leg and climbed into the saddle, then turned Tempest around and urged the horse onward. As she rode, she thought about Copper's story. If he could help her find a way to remove the scale, then perhaps she would change her mind about dragons.

Perhaps she just might befriend one.

14

When Caden came to, he did so with stars bursting across his vision and the worst headache he'd ever experienced. Dawn was cresting on the horizon, and he wondered how long he'd been unconscious.

He was lying face-down on the ground, his left cheek pressed against the dirt. A few rocks were jabbing into his skin, and he could tell his mouth had been open for a while based on the dryness. As he struggled to get up, pain flared across the back of his head and neck.

"Gods," he gasped.

Caden got on his feet and looked at his surroundings. Bodies littered the area, a mix of both friend and foe. The horses that had been attached to the wagon and boxcar were gone. His immediate thought was to search for survivors, but first, he needed water. He walked unsteadily to the remains of the wagon and sifted through the debris until he found a canteen.

Popping the lid off, he drank ravenously. The cool liquid satisfied his parched mouth and throat, but his headache persisted. Caden leaned against the boxcar and waited for his vision to become fully clear, then set about searching the destroyed camp. Their enemy had struck hard and fast, but they hadn't pilfered any of their supplies.

That told Caden that their intent had been solely to kill. He drank some more water and trudged up the hill. There were more bodies at the top, but they were all Lord D'Lance's men. A few hundred feet ahead, an old stone building jutted up from the landscape. It was abandoned, and judging by the overgrowth, nature was doing its best to reclaim the space for itself.

He assumed that's where they were going to leave the dragon, but it didn't make any sense. Nothing did at this point. Caden stared at the structure in silence, trying to piece things together. Movement in the trees caused his heart to leap in his chest. Had the enemy returned to finish him off?

A horse stepped into view, whinnying softly. The leather straps that had bound the creature to the boxcar were present and dangled loosely at its sides.

"A small blessing," Caden whispered.

Lord D'Lance needed to know what had happened here. Another group of men would need to secure the boxcar and get the dragon to her prison. Caden approached the horse and grabbed onto one of the leather straps, then guided the horse down the hill. Oddly, he found it more difficult going down the hill than it had been to go up it.

He looked at the boxcar and paused. The door was lying on the ground, and the interior was empty. The dragon had escaped. Caden hurried as fast as he could the rest of the way down and tied the horse to the tandem pole that was still attached to the boxcar. He realized the door must have been blown off by the ball of flame that had struck it. That was probably what had hit him and knocked him unconscious.

It seemed suspicious to him that their enemies had known they would be here. Had they known they were transporting a dragon? And if so, had they taken it back to Lord Culver's Dominion? The latter thought seemed unlikely. They would've taken the boxcar. There were too many questions, and they only aggravated his headache.

A groan drew his attention and he moved toward the sound. Partially covered by the door of the boxcar was Captain Burke. Caden pulled the metal sheet off the man and looked him over. The captain was wounded. While his injuries didn't appear to be fatal, he wasn't going to be able to walk on his own. Caden knelt beside him.

"Sir? Can you hear me?"

Burke nodded slightly, flinching in pain.

"I found one of the horses, and I'm going to put you on it. It's probably going to hurt."

"Just get it over with," Burke hissed.

"Yes, sir."

Caden slid one arm under Burke's neck and lifted him into a sitting position. Burke's jaw was firmly clenched, and Caden hurriedly removed the man's armor and set it aside. He wasn't sure if his own armor would hinder him, but he took off the breastplate anyway and heaved the captain off the ground.

Despite his short stature, the man was heavier than he looked. Caden's muscled burned as he carried Burke over to the horse. He wasn't sure how he was going to get him on the animal, so he grunted an apology to the captain and essentially threw him into the air. Burke helped by grabbing onto the saddle horn, and between the two of them struggling, managed to get him on the horse's back and somewhat into the saddle.

With Burke situated, Caden turned his attention to the boxcar's door. It wasn't overly heavy, and he had an idea. He cut some of the leather straps from the tandem pole and lashed them together, then tied one end to the saddle and the other to the door. He set Burke's armor on it, as well as his own, and pulled the body of one of their enemies onto it. Now they had proof of who had attacked them, and Lord D'Lance could do as he wished with the information.

All the exertion intensified his headache and he had to rest for a moment to keep from passing out. He steadily downed the water from the canteen he'd found until it was empty, then grabbed the reins and began the trek back to the castle. Burke flitted in and out of consciousness, which forced Caden to rely on his vague memory of the route they'd taken.

His strength gave out on him several times, and he slumped to the ground and waited until his muscles felt rested enough to continue. Caden lost all sense of time, but he knew that he was making progress as he started to recognize landmarks that he'd seen. By the time the castle came into view, the sun was high overhead.

"We made it," Caden said, barely recognizing his own hoarse voice.

He looked over his shoulder and saw that Burke was slumped forward in the saddle. A trail of blood ran from his leg down the side of the horse, and Caden feared that the captain might be dead. Burke's eyes cracked open.

"Find Angus," he said weakly.

Caden wanted nothing more than to lie down and close his eyes, but he knew they would probably both die if he did that. He pushed himself onward, counting his steps as a way of focusing on something other than the pain. They reached the gates and the guards on duty rushed to their aid, one of them sprinting off to find the commander.

Before long, the courtyard was swarming with activity. Leaders were demanding to know what happened, promising retribution. Caden tried to relay the events, but the chaos was too much. He collapsed from exhaustion and was taken to the infirmary. Thankfully, the healers kept anyone from bothering them and Caden was able to rest both his body and his mind. He continuously dozed in and out of sleep until he heard the powerful steps of booted feet.

Commander Morin had arrived, and Lord D'Lance was with him. They spoke with the healers first, then came to stand by his bed.

"Tell me everything," Lord D'Lance demanded.

15

Mina arrived back at Klodian Keep just as the sun was descending. She dismounted Tempest and led the horse to the stable. Aram was still working, and when he saw her, he took the reins from her and led the animal inside.

"I was beginning to get worried," he said.

"You were worried about me?"

"No, I was worried about Tempest. Once the gates close at dark, there's no getting in. I didn't want her being stuck out in the elements all night."

"I wouldn't let that happen," Mina replied. "And even if it did, I would take care of her."

"Be that as it may, I would like all of my horses accounted for before nightfall. I don't ask questions of anyone, but if you can't abide by my rules, I'll have to inform Lord Klodian about your ventures outside the castle. Where do you go, anyway?"

"I just ride around. It relaxes me."

Aram eyed her, and she thought he was going to pursue the conversation. Instead, he shrugged and shooed her out of the stable. Mina went inside the castle and stopped at the dining hall to see if there was any food left. She managed to scrounge up enough scraps to make a full meal and took it up to her room.

She was supposed to meet Thais at midnight,

and she was thoroughly exhausted. She was tempted to send word to the Runesman that they would try tomorrow night instead but getting the egg to Copper was too important. It guaranteed that he would help her find a way to remove the scale, and she wanted that above all else. Sleep would have to wait.

Mina entered her room and sat on the bed as she wolfed down her food. She wondered if Thais had come up with a suitable diversion. If not, then they would simply have to improvise. And then there was the issue of the mysterious couple intent on overthrowing Klodian. Mina decided to leave that problem to Thais. She had enough on her plate with stealing the egg.

After she finished eating, she laid down and stared up at the ceiling. Her stomach was full, and her exhaustion seemed to intensify. She yawned and fought to keep her eyes open but fell asleep anyway. She startled awake from a nightmare and looked to the window. It was dark.

"Blast it," she muttered.

A glance at the water clock revealed it was just after midnight. Mina cursed and clambered off the bed, rushing out of the room and through the halls. The castle was quiet, and Mina didn't encounter anyone except a few guards who were walking their rounds. They took an interest in her until they realized who she was, then they ignored her and went about their business.

Mina left the castle and looked around the

courtyard. She didn't see Thais. The woman had probably gotten tired of waiting on her and returned to the barracks.

"Over here!" A voice whispered harshly.

Mina peered at the shadows that veiled the side of the castle. Hidden among them was Thais. She stepped into the light and frowned.

"You're late."

"Sorry. I fell asleep."

"Must be nice. Are we still doing this or what?"

"Yes, of course. I like the servant's robes you're wearing. That should help us avoid any unwanted attention. Does it have a hood?"

In reply, Thais reached back and pulled a hood over her head, hiding her face.

"Follow me," Mina said.

She led Thais into the castle, keeping her pace quick. Instead of going forward through the maze of hallways, she turned to the left and headed down the stairwell that led to the lower level of the castle.

"Have you been to the dungeon before?"

"No," Thais replied.

"The room we need to get inside of is just before the dungeon, so there will probably be a few guards. What did you come up with as a diversion?"

"I'm still working on that. You didn't give me much time to prepare, and my thoughts have been preoccupied with my duties."

"As long as no one sees me go into the room, everything should be fine. You just need to get the attention off me."

"For how long?" Thais asked.

"A few minutes. I know the egg is in there, I just don't know exactly where it's kept."

"What egg?"

Mina sucked in a breath, realizing her mistake. She ignored the question and continued down the stairs. They reached the bottom and Thais looked at her expectantly.

"I told you before, I'll explain everything if we pull this off."

"Yeah, yeah. Which way?"

Two hallways branched off from the landing, one to the left and the other straight on.

"I'm not sure where that leads to," Mina said, motioning to the left corridor. "We're going this way."

They continued onward and Mina froze when she heard voices. There was no sign of anyone ahead, and she quickly realized the voices were coming from one of the rooms. Mina motioned for Thais to follow her, and the two walked quietly.

"Changes are coming to the Thophate, whether you like them or not. If you want to be included in those changes, you would do well to align yourself with the right people."

Mina recognized the voice as the man she'd

overheard speaking about overthrowing Klodian. Her heart started racing, and she turned to Thais.

"That's one of them," she whispered.

"Who?"

"The two people I told you about that mentioned the spy. That's the man."

"Who is he talking to?" Thais asked.

"I don't know."

Mina stepped closer to the doorway and slowly tilted her head to look inside. The door was ajar, but not enough for her to see the man who was speaking.

"You said that Lord D'Lance has evidence of a crime. What crime are you talking about?" It was Captain Eduard's voice.

Mina and Thais exchanged looks.

"Treason against the High Prince," the man answered. "Lord Klodian is involved in a plot with Lord Culver. They seek to start a war."

"What is he talking about?" Thais scowled. "Lord Klodian isn't potting anything."

"Not that we know of," Mina said. "He's been absent for a while now."

"He's not in the castle?"

"He is, but he's been in his personal chamber, sealed off from everything. I haven't seen him since he gave me my freedom."

"That doesn't mean he's involved in anything nefarious."

"Not necessarily, but who's to say?"

"My loyalty lies with the Dominion," Captain Eduard said. "Who rules from its throne doesn't matter to me."

"I'll take that as a promise of support, and I'll be sure that Lord D'Lance rewards you for your service. In the end, keeping the High Prince safe is the ultimate goal. I will call upon you when the time is right. Until then, it's business as usual. I appreciate your time, captain."

Mina grabbed Thais's arm and pulled her toward the door on the other side of the hall. They entered the room and Mina kept the door cracked, peering out into the hall. She saw Captain Eduard exit the room and close the door behind him. He headed for the stairs, a troubled look on his face.

"I don't think the captain is happy about what he's been told," Mina said.

"That's not surprising. He's loyal to the Dominion, but he's also loyal to Lord Klodian. I don't know what our mystery man is up to, but it can't be good."

"He's going to overthrow Lord Klodian, but it sounds like someone else is behind it. Who is Lord D'Lance?"

"He's the top dog among the Dominion Lords. He commands more soldiers than anyone other than the High Prince himself. Is there anyone else in that room with him?"

"I'm not sure," Mina replied. "I only heard Captain Eduard."

"We should confront him, find out what's going on."

"No. We need to keep to the plan."

"Plans change," Thais said, her tone giddy. "We can unravel all of this right now."

Before Mina could argue with her, Thais opened the door and strode across the hall.

"Stop!"

Thais didn't pay her any heed. She pushed through the other door and went inside. There was a shout, followed by a crash. Mina swallowed hard and peered down the hall toward the dungeon, fearing that the guards would come to investigate. Silence settled over the hall, and no guards came. Thais appeared in the doorway.

"Get in here," she said.

Mina hurried across the hall and followed her into the room. A man was sprawled on the floor, unconscious.

"What did you do?" Mina demanded.

"I'm protecting Lord Klodian. If this man is a spy, we can get the answers we need from him."

"How?"

Thais smirked. "By torturing him, of course."

Mina looked from the prone man to Thais and back again. She had the sinking feeling that she wasn't going to get her hands on the egg tonight.

"His friend will know he's missing. The woman."

"Then we'll leave a note for her to find that says he needed to leave. This is important. More important than your egg, whatever that is. Unless you care to reveal the details about that now?"

Mina chewed on her lower lip. She needed Thais's help to get the egg, but she didn't trust the woman enough to tell her anything. There was also the fact that despite Copper's friendly demeanor, he could just be using her. And there was Lord Klodian, the only man strong enough to kill a dragon on his own. There was too much going on.

"I'll help you if you swear that we'll get the egg tomorrow night."

"We will. On my word as a Runesman."

"Fine." Mina looked down at the man. "What do we do with him?"

16

After Caden had relayed what little he remembered about the attack, Lord D'Lance and Commander Morin left him to rest. A healer approached his bed, smiling warmly. She was dressed in white robes and had striking blue eyes.

"How are you feeling?" she asked.

"My head is pounding," he replied.

"You do have some head trauma. And you were also burned. It's a miracle you even survived, let alone were able to make it back to the castle."

Caden was surprised by her words. He'd felt rough, but he hadn't thought that his injuries should have killed him. He considered himself lucky.

"I've got a salve that will help with the burn, but it's going to cause you some pain when I apply it."

"I think I can handle it."

The healer helped him to roll onto his side, and then her soft hands gently touched his skin. A wave of pain washed over him, and his eyes rolled into the back of his head. When he awoke, he was lying on his back again. The pain of the burn had lessened, but his headache remained the same, a constant throbbing in the back of his skull.

"Soldier." It was Burke.

Caden sat himself up and saw that the captain

was a few beds down, on the same row as himself.

"Sir?"

"Thank you for saving my life."

"I was just doing my duty, sir."

"Maybe so, but not many men have the fortitude you displayed. I saw the back of your head and thought you were going to die on me. I'm glad to see you're still here."

"It'll take more than a headwound to take me out, sir," Caden said.

Burke chuckled, then went silent for a long moment.

"You've done more than I could expect, but I'm afraid I must ask more from you."

"What do you need me to do?"

Burke glanced at the healers in the room. "I'll tell you tonight."

Judging by the captain's demeanor, Caden knew it must be something secretive. Now that his curiosity was piqued, he was impatient for the time to pass. He laid back down and tried to rest, but his mind was too alert. He replayed the events of the night before. The robed man who had thrown the fireballs had been using magic. Magic that was banned by decree of the High Prince.

If Lord Culver was truly trying to cause a war, his actions last night would certainly be the catalyst. Caden remembered what Thais had told him, about her father being killed in battle. Lord Culver called him a failure and banished Thais and her mother from his Dominion. The man was a lawless monster.

The hours passed monotonously, aside from the healers who came to apply salve to his burn or bring him food. His headache eventually faded to a minor pulsing, and he spent some of the time cleaning the dirt from under his nails. As the sunlight flowing through the windows began to dim, one of the healers came to see him.

"Given the nature of your wounds, we're going to keep you here for the night. We don't expect you to have any issues, but there will be someone on duty. If you start to feel bad in any way, ring the bell by the door."

"Thank you," Caden said. "Do you think I'll be able to leave in the morning?"

"That remains to be seen. We don't want you to aggravate your injuries, so we're going to take it one day at a time."

While Caden didn't like the idea of lying around for days on end, he also didn't want to disrupt his healing. He watched the healer leave the infirmary, then turned his attention to Burke. The captain had his eyes closed and appeared to be sleeping. Once nightfall had fully descended, Burke called his name.

"Come over here."

Caden eased himself off the bed and slowly walked to where Burke was. The captain's midsection was wrapped in bandages. A spot on his ribcage had blood leaking through, but it wasn't enough to cause worry.

"I can't move around much," Burke said. "Are we alone?"

Caden didn't see anyone, but he walked around the room just to be certain.

"All clear."

"Good. I need you to return to the site of our attack and look for anything out of the ordinary."

Caden's scrunched his face, which caused a brief lance of pain to shoot through his neck.

"I need you to trust me. Something isn't right about that ambush."

"What do you mean? Hasn't Lord Culver been trying to start a war? Attacking us would bring Lord D'Lance's wrath down on him, which will probably lead to war. He's signed his own death warrant."

"That's the problem," Burke said, lowering his voice. "I don't think Lord Culver is behind this."

"Why not?"

"I served under Lord Culver for a while before transferring here a few years ago. Lord Culver is one of the most honorable men I've ever known. When I saw his emblem on the armor of the soldiers who attacked us, it didn't sit right with me."

"People change," Caden replied. "He may not be the man you once knew."

"People *can* change, but I don't think Lord Culver would become a tyrant. His Dominion is closest to the High Prince and has long been coveted by the other Dominion Lords."

He didn't name off anyone specific, but Caden took the hint.

"Why would Lord D'Lance want Culver's Dominion? He's got more soldiers and land here."

"It's not about the size, but the location. Lord Culver's Dominion is the only thing that stands in the way of an army and the High Prince."

"If someone was going to attack the High Prince, they would have to come through all of the Dominions first," Caden argued. "They wouldn't make it very far."

"Unless the attacker is a Dominion Lord."

Caden opened his mouth to reply and paused. The captain had a valid point.

"You think Lord D'Lance is trying to make it look like Lord Culver is stirring up trouble so he can take over his Dominion?"

Burke nodded mutely.

"For what purpose?"

"Who knows, though I have my suspicions," Burke replied. "Our loyalties are with our Dominion lord, but ultimately they rest with the High Prince. If there is nothing at the ambush site to indicate what I'm saying is true, then we have nothing to be concerned about. However, if there is, then I fear we must get word to the High Prince immediately."

Caden agreed that the picture Burke painted was troubling.

"Is there something specific I should be looking for? And what about the dragon? What if it's still out there?"

"The dragon will be long gone, I'm sure. Just check the bodies. If they truly are Lord Culver's Runesmen, they'll bear his rune. That's the only thing that I can think of."

"I'll go first thing in the morning," Caden said.

"No, you must leave tonight. If I'm correct, then time is something we don't have enough of."

"Tonight? I barely walked in a straight line to your bed. There's no way I can make it to that far on foot."

"You won't have to."

Burke extended his hand and held up a small pin. It had Lord D'Lance's emblem engraved on the front.

"This will give you access to everything I have as a captain, including a horse. That will allow you to get there and return before morning."

Caden felt as though he were somehow working behind Lord D'Lance's back. The man had accepted him and even offered him the opportunity to earn the fame and fortune he wanted.

"I don't know if I can do this," Caden said.

"There is no else. We were the only ones who saw what happened and lived. I can't walk at all, so it must be you."

Caden wanted to say no. He wanted to forget everything Burke had told him and serve Lord D'Lance without question. But he couldn't, not until his mind was eased of the doubts Burke had instilled.

Caden took the pin.

17

After Mina and Thais had bound and gagged their prisoner, they'd snuck him into one of the cells in the dungeon for safekeeping. Thais had penned a letter since she knew how to write, and Mina had delivered it to the man's partner, slipping it under the door of their chamber.

Mina wasn't sure if the woman would believe that her co-conspirator would suddenly be called away, but Thais had convinced her that it was the most logical excuse for his absence. She then helped Thais out of the castle and returned to her room and managed to get a few hours of sleep.

A faint light shone through her windows as dawn arrived, and she forced herself out of bed. She didn't have to visit Copper this early, but she wanted to be certain she'd return before nightfall. Thais had mentioned interrogating their prisoner, but Mina refused to do anything until she had the egg in her hands.

She went down to the dining hall and ate a quick breakfast, then headed for the stable. Aram was absent, but a younger man was there shoveling out the stalls. Mina asked for Tempest, and the man handed the horse over without any questions. It was curious that Aram wasn't working, but she assumed he needed a break as much as anyone else.

Mina left the castle behind and guided Tempest

toward the mesa where she'd been meeting with Copper. She had grown accustomed to constantly feeling his presence through the scale. Regardless of the distance between them, he was always there. It was another mystery that she hoped to unravel.

Tempest slowed as they reached the mesa and began to whinny, jerking her head against the reins. Mina patted the horse's neck comfortingly and scanned the sky. Atop the mesa, she could see Copper's head as he peered down at her.

I see you have returned without the egg, his voice rumbled in her mind.

Yes. Things didn't go according to plan.

Do you want me to bring you up here?

Mina hesitated. It was certainly quicker than climbing, but it was also terrifying. She debated back and forth with herself before Copper's chortling laughter interrupted her thoughts.

What?

I had forgotten how humans think. It's quite entertaining, really.

You can hear my thoughts?

Sometimes, Copper answered. *When you are close as you are now. It is more difficult when you are further away.*

Mina abruptly felt self-conscious. Had he heard all of her thoughts during their last encounter? Was he hearing them now? She shook her head, trying to clear her mind, and guided Tempest to a stop. She slid out of the saddle and walked around the mesa wall until Tempest was no longer visible.

A whooshing sound filled the air and Copper landed on the ground ahead of her. His wings were stretched out, and as Mina approached him, she could see the light shining through the membrane of his wings, highlighting veins and small punctures.

Do those holes affect your ability to fly? she asked.

No.

How did you get them?

Battles, mostly.

With other dragons?

A few of them, yes.

Mina extended her arms and tried to remain calm. Copper leaped into the air and flapped his wings, grabbing hold of her and lifting her into the air. The instinct to scream clawed at her mind as it had the first time, but she kept her mouth clamped shut. Her feet touched the ground again and she heaved in a relieved breath. Copper's wings stirred up the dust, causing Mina to cough as it got into her nose and mouth. Once it settled, Copper stared at her intently.

What happened with the egg?

The person I had asked to help me ruined my plan. She was supposed to draw attention so that I could get into the room and steal it.

Does she know what you are after?

No. Mina remembered her slip-up and corrected herself. *Well, I don't think so.*

Did she try to sabotage you?

Not intentionally. There is something I didn't mention yesterday. I overheard two people talking about overthrowing Lord Klodian. They also mentioned a spy being in the castle, and when I told her about them, she wanted to find out who they are. When we went down to get the egg, one of them was down there, a man. Thais knocked him out and now we have him in the dungeon.

It seems she has different priorities. Is she the best suited to help you?

She's the only one who can *help me,* Mina said. *I'll have to help her before she'll help me, but she wants to interrogate the man.*

What's the problem?

She's a soldier and she isn't allowed in the castle. I had to sneak her in last night, but if she gets caught, she'll be in trouble and I'll lose my help.

Copper hummed. The sound sent gentle vibrations through the ground that reached Mina's toes despite her boots, and it tickled her. She shifted her stance and clenched her feet against the feeling.

Perhaps I can help you, he finally said.

How?

I can search his mind.

Truly?

We dragons can do many things. The scale in your leg will provide the means, but you must touch the man.

In the back of her mind, Mina wondered if Copper was telling the truth. She trusted Thais more than she did the dragon, but if he was able to do what he said, then whatever he learned would hopefully placate Thais.

It's worth trying, she admitted.

When can you speak to this man? I will need to be close to you for this to work, and if I am seen near the castle during daylight, there are bound to be problems.

I can go at night. Will that work?

Yes. It will be easier to hide in the darkness.

Then it's settled, Mina said. *I'll go at midnight. Most of the servants will be asleep, and there shouldn't be many guards on the walls.*

Very well. Copper lifted his head and sniffed the air, growling lowly.

What is it?

A sand wyrm is nearby.

Mina tensed and looked around.

You are safe up here, Copper said. *They cannot burrow through the rock. It is curious that one is so far from the deeper area of the desert.*

What about my horse?

Copper turned his gaze on her.

You should go.

Mina swallowed hard, a wave of fear washing over her. She had no idea what a sand wyrm was, nor what one looked like, but her instincts told her she needed to run.

Will it follow me?

If it catches your scent. You'll need to ride fast.

I had hoped to spend more time with you. I have so many questions.

Your questions will have to wait, though I will answer one on the way down.

Copper launched himself into the air and Mina held her arms out, and then she was dropping toward the ground. She struggled to get her thoughts in order but managed to decide on the most pressing question.

Why can I feel you in the scale at all times?

They swooped down the side of the mesa, and Mina watched as the wall sped past. She was on the ground before she had time to realize it.

As you put it, there is something I haven't told you, Copper said. *I recognize the scale in your leg now.*

You know whose it is?

Yes.

Tell me!

The scent of lavender filled her nostrils, and she wondered why the dragon was afraid. He couldn't be afraid of her, could he? Or was he afraid that she would lead Lord Klodian to the dragon?

It is mine.

Mina was speechless. She stared at Copper with wide eyes. How was that possible? Her family's farm was many miles from Lord Klodian's castle. If the dragons resided among The Long Sands, how would one of Copper's scales have gotten in the nest near the farm?

You must go! Now!

The ground shook beneath Mina's feet, and she heard Tempest cry out in alarm. She sprinted around the mesa and saw the ground heaving up as something under the sand approached. Tempest's eyes were wild with terror.

"Please don't run," Mina prayed as she ran toward the horse.

She got her foot in the stirrup and was swinging her leg up over the saddle just as Tempest bolted. Mina held onto the reins as tightly as she could and tried to situate herself. Copper took to the air, causing Tempest to change directions. They were now in between the dragon and the sand wyrm.

Go left! Copper shouted in her mind.

She jerked the reins in reply, hoping the horse would obey. Tempest followed her lead and adjusted course. The sand wyrm also changed direction and broke the surface of the sand. The creature rose up, up, up into the air, the muscles of its long body undulating. It had no eyes that Mina could see, but it had an enormous circular mouth filled with serrated teeth. It twisted in the air toward her and Tempest.

Mina screamed.

18

Caden thundered along the road astride a well-muscled destrier. The horse was doubtless more valuable than he was. When he'd asked the stable hand for a quick horse, he hadn't expected to be given such a magnificent animal. He *had* anticipated questions, but when he flashed the pin, no one asked him anything.

The lack of security was both a blessing and a concern. Regardless, he continuously questioned himself about why he was going through with Burke's request. A part of him argued that it was because Burke was a captain, and since he was a superior, Caden had to oblige the man.

And yet, there was something about Burke's words that bothered Caden. If the captain was right about the ambush, and Lord D'Lance's ulterior motives toward Lord Culver, then Caden was going to be drawn into something he wanted no part of. Saving the High Prince from being overthrown, or worse, would surely get him a reward, but nothing worth doing was ever easy, at least in his experience.

The distance flew by quickly, and when he reached the campsite, he was confused. There were no bodies, no boxcar, nothing. He dismounted from the horse and walked around the area. Overhead, the sky was clear and the moon shined brightly, giving him plenty of light to see by. Perhaps he was in the wrong spot? Everything looked familiar, though, even the burn marks on the ground and the trees.

Caden walked up the hill and saw the stone building. He was in the right spot. Why had everything been cleaned up already? He supposed Lord D'Lance wouldn't want word of what happened to get out, but if Burke's suspicions were true …

"I've got a bad feeling about this," Caden muttered.

He spent some time searching the area, looking for anything that may have been missed by whoever had cleaned the place. His headache returned, and he decided to go back to the castle. It was suspicious that there was nothing that remained, but he would let Burke know and let the captain decide what he wanted to do. Caden had done his duty, and he was going to wash his hands of the situation and pretend he didn't have his doubts.

The sun was creeping over the horizon when he arrived at the castle. He returned the horse to the stables and hurried toward the infirmary, but paused when something occurred to him. He'd brought back one of the enemy's bodies. If there were any clues to be had, perhaps he'd find them on the body. There was just one problem. He didn't know where it had been taken.

Caden turned away from the infirmary and backtracked, returning to the main entrance. Despite the early hour, many people were coming and going through the castle. He stopped someone on a whim, flashing the pin nonchalantly.

"Perhaps you can help me. Two Runesmen returned this morning with a tale of being ambushed. Do you know what I'm referring to?"

"The attack perpetrated by Lord Culver? Yeah, I heard about it. Who hasn't?"

"They brought back a body with them of one of the attackers. Do you know what they did with it?"

"It was paraded around the grounds earlier. Commander Morin said that was all the proof we needed to end Lord Culver's attempted campaign against the High Prince. Lord D'Lance has practically declared war."

"Do you know where the body is now?"

"At the chapel, last I heard. Though if you ask me, no enemy of ours deserves a proper funeral."

"Where is the chapel?"

"It's on the west side of the castle, near the barracks for the regular soldiers."

Caden thanked the man and rushed through the halls, frantically looking for the chapel and praying that the body hadn't already been buried. He entered a section that was separated from the main castle, though connected structurally by a covered walkway. The morning air was chill, and it drove back the heat that Caden felt flushing his face.

The chapel doors were propped open, and he stepped inside. The interior reminded him of the infirmary. Everything was white, crisp, and clean.

Clergy members wearing white robes were offering prayers and speaking with people privately. The pews were empty, and Caden doubted that the morning service had begun yet.

He approached one of the clerics, a young woman with short brown hair. He'd confused her for a man at first and almost called her 'sir' before catching himself.

"Good morning," she greeted. "How may I help you?"

"I was told the body of a soldier was brought here. Is it still here?"

"Do you mean Lord Culver's soldier or another?"

"Yes, that's the one. Is it still here?"

"It is. If Lord D'Lance has sent you to tell us to dispose of it, tell your lord that the Church will not be bullied into submission. We will perform the necessary rituals, and then we will bury him."

So, Lord D'Lance had told them to get rid of the body. Why would he do that unless there was something to hide?

"I'm here of my own volition," Caden replied. "I need to check the body for … something."

"What is the reason that you must disturb the dead? There is enough suffering in life that the dead should be left alone."

"I wouldn't ask if it wasn't important. Please."

The woman stared at him in silence for a long

moment, then nodded. "Very well."

She led him to the back of the chapel and through a door that opened into a large vaulted room. A number of bodies were laid out on stone slabs, covered with thin white shrouds.

"You are lucky that the prayers for the dead have not begun, else we would not allow you in here. This is the one," she said as they stopped at one of the slabs.

Caden pulled the shroud back. The man's armor had been removed, revealing a young face. The man couldn't have been much older than himself. His eyes had been closed, and his expression was one of peace. Caden lifted his head, but he couldn't get a good look at the rune, so he turned the man onto his side. The rune was the same as the one he'd seen on the emblem. A clawed paw print surrounded by a blazing sun.

Caden breathed a sigh of relief. Burke had been wrong. This was indeed one of Lord Culver's men. He started to roll the body onto its back when he spotted something covering the bottom of the rune. He leaned closer, but he couldn't determine what it was, so he rubbed his finger across it and held it up.

"What is it?" the cleric asked.

"I think it's ink," he replied. "Do you have a cloth?"

"No."

Caden grabbed the edge of the shroud and wiped the rune with the material. To his horror, the ink came right off, revealing a different rune underneath. Lord D'Lance's rune.

"You're certain this is the same body that was brought here this morning?"

"Yes."

"How certain?"

Her look of disapproval told him everything he needed to know. He pulled the shroud back over the body and left the chapel, heading back into the castle. Why was one of Lord D'Lance's Runesmen wearing a fake rune? The answer hovered in the back of his mind, but he didn't want to accept it. Burke had been right.

Caden rushed into the infirmary, ready to tell the captain what he'd discovered. A group of healers had gathered around Burke's bed, but he couldn't see what they were doing.

"What's going on?" he asked.

"There you are," one of them said. "We've been looking all over for you."

"I'm fine. What's wrong with Captain Burke?"

The healer cast her eyes to the floor forlornly. "He's dead."

19

Tempest reared back on her hind legs and Mina almost fell out of the saddle. She wrapped her arms around the horse's neck and prepared to die.

An unearthly roar split the air, and Mina watched in awe as Copper dropped from the sky. His talons raked along the sand wyrm's fleshy body, rending deep wounds that quickly filled with black blood.

The creature issued a horrendous shriek that made Mina think her eardrums were going to burst. Copper dug his talons into the wyrm's body and flapped his wings, pulling the behemoth away from Mina and her mount.

Flee! Copper shouted.

Mina released Tempest's neck and pulled on the reins, urging the horse to move. At first, she thought Tempest wasn't going to obey her, but the animal backed up a few steps and then hurtled in the direction of the castle. Mina rode hard, not daring to look back, even after they reached the castle. She knew it was irrational that she would see the two monsters battling at this distance, but she was terrified.

She returned Tempest to the stable and rushed through the castle, escaping to her room where she let tears flow freely down her face. Her emotions mingled together, overwhelming her, and she sat on the floor near her bed and sobbed. She had nearly died, out in the middle of the desert where no one would have seen anything except Copper.

Copper.

He'd saved her life. A dragon, of all things. And then she remembered what he'd said. It was *his* scale in her leg. She considered the implications and began to suspect that their meeting in the mesa that day with Lord Klodian might not have been a coincidence. That didn't explain why Vhan had been killed by his brethren, but it gave her something to consider.

Her focus switched from the sand wyrm to Copper, and she managed to calm herself. Mina wiped the tears from her face and stood, glancing to the window. She touched the scale in her leg and could feel Copper's presence, though she couldn't hear his voice. Perhaps later, when he was close enough, she would get answers to some of her questions.

For now, she would have to let Thais know that there had been a change in plans. Mina checked her appearance in the mirror and fixed her hair, then left her room and made her way to the barracks. The place was empty, so Mina walked the courtyard searching for Thais, but the woman was nowhere to be found. She looked at the gates, wondering if she was out on patrol.

"Mina."

Although she was no longer a slave, Lord Klodian's voice still had the same effect on her. Her heart skipped a beat and she turned around. He was walking with Captain Eduard and he motioned for her to come near.

"It is good to see you, my Lord. I've been wondering when you would come calling for me."

"I've been busy dealing with some things," he replied.

"Are we going on a hunt?" she asked.

"No, I don't have time for that right now."

Mina was relieved to hear that.

"We have a problem. Lord Burgess has gone missing, and his wife is distraught. She said she received a letter saying he was being called away, but it wasn't in his handwriting. Have you seen or heard anything?"

"No, my Lord. Perhaps he had one of the servants write it for him?"

"We've questioned the servants," Eduard said. "All of them. Unless one of them is lying, no one was asked to pen anything for him."

"I'll let you know if I hear anything," Mina replied.

Lord Klodian nodded, but Mina noticed that he appeared to be distracted. He started to walk off, then looked at her.

"The stablemaster told me you've been borrowing a horse?"

"Yes, my Lord. The rides help to clear my

mind."

"Of what?"

"The dragons. I feel as though I sense them all the time lately, ever since Vhan …" Mina trailed off, hoping he would change the subject.

Lord Klodian cleared his throat. "Yes, it was unfortunate that he was killed. The dragons responsible will pay with their blood." Lord Klodian swept his gaze across the courtyard. "Keep your ears open and let me know if you hear anything about Lord Burgess's disappearance."

"I will, my Lord."

The two men left and she returned to her room. Thais wouldn't like being left out, but Mina was just going to have to go through with letting Copper probe Lord Burgess's mind. Now that his absence had stirred suspicion, she needed to hurry. In the back of her mind, the question of what to do with him after interrogating him continued to berate her. She would simply have to figure things out, as she always did.

When evening came, Mina was pacing her room. She could hear people in the hall retiring for the night, and her impatience was hard to contain. It wasn't just about getting the egg. She wanted to speak with Copper.

The clouds are thick tonight, his voice said, interrupting her thoughts. *That will help hide me.*

I wondered if you were still going to come, Mina replied.

I said I would, and I am a dragon of my word.

Are you all right? Did the sand wyrm hurt you?

Copper laughed. *No, it did not hurt me. They might be bigger, but they are slow, lumbering creatures compared to us dragons.*

I thought I was going to die.

You could have.

You saved me ... why?

Copper fell silent, and Mina wondered if he would refuse to answer.

I don't know how, but I believe you and I are bonded. I felt it first in the mesa with my brethren, but I wasn't sure if I imagined the feeling. Each time we talk, I feel it more strongly. When I saw the sand wyrm coming for you, I couldn't allow you to die. It would have been easier that way, but it would not have been right.

When you say bonded, what do you mean? Like the humans and dragons before?

Yes

Mina paused mid-step in her pacing. She couldn't believe it. She didn't want to, and yet, it explained her ability to sense dragons. It wasn't the scale itself, but the bond between her and Copper that enabled it.

I fell on this scale near my parents' home. How is it that your scale would end up there if you live in the desert?

When we mate, we leave the desert to find more hospitable areas for our eggs. The heat is too much for the unhatched to handle. You must have fallen into one of my old nests.

Copper was the dragon responsible for the way her life had changed. She had spent so many years full of hatred, and now that she knew who the scale belonged to, she found it difficult to hold onto that hate. What was wrong with her? What had changed?

Is that why you were afraid?

Dragons fear nothing.

Mina smiled. She knew better than to believe that.

Are you near the prisoner? He asked.

No. I'm waiting for the servants to retire. It should be safe to see him shortly. While we wait, can you answer some questions?

I will try.

Since we are connected by this bond, will I be able to speak to you if the scale is removed?

Yes, though I am not sure how the bond was created in the first place. I spoke with my brethren about removing your scale, but there is no clear answer on how it can be done. I fear that it may kill you to do so.

Mina didn't want to risk her life to remove it. And there didn't seem to be much point in removing it now if she would still be able to sense dragons. There had to be a way to block them out somehow.

There is, Copper said. *I can teach you if you want.*

I would like that, Mina replied. *It would be nice to keep you from hearing my personal thoughts. Some things are just private.*

She looked at the water clock. The servants would be done with their duties now.

It's time.

20

Caden was confused. "Dead? How?"

"He succumbed to his wounds not long ago."

Burke had been wounded, but he didn't think the wound hadn't been life-threatening. He watched as the healers lifted the captain's body off the bed and onto a stretcher, then they carried him out of the infirmary. The host of healers dispersed, and Caden stood alone staring at the empty bed.

Something wasn't right. Burke had been fine earlier. He walked over to the bed and noticed a piece of parchment sticking out from under the pillow. Scrawled roughly on it was written the words:

Don't trust anyone.

He crumpled the paper and looked around the infirmary. If Burke had been killed, it was probably at Lord D'Lance's command. At least, that was his suspicion. Perhaps his mind was clouded by Burke's words … but that wouldn't explain the false rune on the dead soldier. Everything that Burke had said appeared to be true, and that meant he had no one to turn to. Before he could decide his next steps, Commander Morin strode into the infirmary.

"I just got word about Captain Burke. To say I'm surprised would be an understatement. His wounds didn't seem that serious."

Caden nodded silently.

"How are you feeling?"

"I still have some pain, but I'll recover."

"Good, good. Lord D'Lance has requested to see you in the Cathedra."

"Now, sir?" Caden asked.

"Yes, unless you aren't feeling up to it. Should I call one of the healers for you?"

"No, I'm fine. I just have a lot on my mind, sir."

"Looking death in the face can be traumatic. It leaves you questioning things. Don't be afraid of those questions, embrace them. It'll make you stronger." He paused. "We should get moving. Lord D'Lance is waiting."

Angus escorted Caden in silence to the Coterie, where a small host of people were waiting to get an audience. The guards let them pass without question, and they entered the Cathedra. Lord D'Lance was sitting on his throne listening to two men dressed in extravagant clothing. Upon seeing them, Lord D'Lance held up his hand and the men fell silent.

"I apologize, gentlemen, but we will have to reconvene. I have pressing matters to attend to."

The men bowed low and left, whispering to one another. Angus waved for Caden to follow him and they approached the throne, stopping at the edge of the purple rug. Caden didn't wait to follow Angus's lead. He knelt and bowed his head.

"Rise," Lord D'Lance said.

Caden stood up and turned his gaze upon the Dominion Lord. He remained sitting, and the gold trim of his robes shimmered in the light that slanted in through the myriad of windows that ringed the top of the Cathedra.

"How are you feeling?"

The question was innocent, but his voice made Caden squirm uncomfortably.

"I was wounded, but it's nothing I can't push through, my Lord."

"I'm glad that you were able to deliver the news of the attack to us. It couldn't have been easy riding through the night while helping Captain Burke. You are to be commended for your fortitude."

"Thank you, my Lord. I was merely doing my duty."

Lord D'Lance turned his attention to Angus. "What of the captain? Is it true?"

"Yes, I'm afraid so."

"I see. It seems we are in need of a new captain. Any candidates in mind, commander?"

"Only one that I can think of."

They both turned their eyes on Caden. He swallowed hard to clear his throat which had suddenly become constricted.

"What do you say, Caden? You came here seeking fame and fortune, and you've proven yourself a capable Runesman. How do you feel about a promotion?"

"I'm not sure that I'm ready for that yet," Caden replied. It was a lie, of course. He was ready to lead, but he didn't know what to do with the information he'd learned from Burke. He couldn't trust Lord D'Lance, or Angus for that matter.

"Those meant to lead usually aren't ready, but it's not about being ready," Angus said. "It's about taking the opportunity."

"I've received reports that Lord Culver has an army at the border," Lord D'Lance said. "He's preparing to enter the Dracan Dominion at any moment, and I need someone capable to lead the Runesmen I'm sending there. Do you want the promotion?"

Caden considered the offer. It would allow him to confirm whether Lord Culver was truly responsible for everything, but it also posed a risk. If it was a trap like the dragon escort was, then he might not make it out alive. Though if it was a trap, he'd be prepared this time and he could flee to Lord Culver's Dominion and tell him everything Lord D'Lance had done.

"If you think I am the best suited, then I accept," Caden said. "When do we leave for the border?"

Lord D'Lance rose from his throne. "In a few hours, so you'll need to get some rest. Before you do, you need to take my rune." He snapped his fingers and one of the guards standing beside the throne stepped forward. "I need a scribe."

The soldier saluted and rushed off.

"Will having two different runes be a problem?" Caden asked.

"It shouldn't. Lord Klodian is too far from here to utilize the magic, so it won't interfere with my rune."

"If Lord Klodian was within distance, what would happen if both of you tried to use your runes at the same time?"

"It would probably kill you," Lord D'Lance replied. "Don't concern yourself with such things. I only use my Runesmen if it is important. And as I said, Lord Klodian is too far away. The chances of both of us trying to borrow your strength at the same time is slim."

Slim, but not impossible, Caden thought. The soldier returned a moment later, and an older man with gray hair followed quickly behind him. He carried a wooden tray that was covered with utensils and vials.

"My Lord," the scribe greeted, stopping to kneel.

"Please put my rune on him," Lord D'Lance instructed, motioning to Caden.

The scribe eyed Caden for a moment, then turned to Lord D'Lance. "Strength rune, yes?"

"Astute, as always master scribe. You are correct."

"Come over here and sit on the floor," the old

man said.

Caden did as he asked, moving off the rug to sit on the stone floor. The scribe had him move around until the light from the windows was just right, then he told Caden to remove his shirt. He obeyed, and the scribe cleared his throat.

"He has a rune already, my Lord."

"Yes, I'm aware. Put mine below it."

"Very well. I assume you want me to cut this other one?"

"No. Leave it be."

Caden noticed that the scribe hesitated, but he nodded and began his work. The pinprick of the scribe's utensils didn't hurt much, but the hunched position he was sitting in made his back ache. When the scribe was finally done, Caden groaned in relief as he sat up straight and stretched his muscles.

"Let me see it," Lord D'Lance said.

Caden stood and turned around.

"Perfect. You are dismissed."

The scribe placed everything on his tray and left. Caden gingerly put his shirt back on.

"Return to the barracks and get some rest. Commander Morin will fill you in on the way."

"Yes, my Lord."

Caden left the Cathedra and headed for the barracks, slowly forming a plan in his mind. This would be the perfect opportunity to find out what was really going on.

21

The halls were empty as Mina made her way into the lower part of the castle. The door to the room where Thais had waylaid Lord Burgess was wide open, but there was no one inside. Mina walked quietly, constantly looking over her shoulder.

If you are no longer a slave, why are you afraid of being caught? Copper asked.

It's hard to explain.

She reached the dungeon and paused outside the door, listening for voices. She could hear people talking, but they didn't sound close. Mina pushed the door open and slipped across the threshold. Only a handful of torches provided light, and the air felt heavy.

They had left the door to Lord Burgess's cell unlocked, seeing as how they didn't have the keys, but he'd been bound tightly so that he couldn't move. Mina crept up to the cell and peered into the darkness. Lord Burgess was still there, but he wasn't moving. She had the sudden fear that Thais may have killed him, but as she stepped into the cell, she heard his low moans.

What do I need to do? she asked.

Touch his head and clear your mind. I'll do the rest.

Mina knelt beside Lord Burgess and he looked up at her. He struggled against his bonds and tried to speak, but the gag in his mouth made the words come out as muffled groans. Mina hesitantly placed her hand on his forehead and closed her eyes. She allowed the darkness to envelop her, and she emptied her mind.

Copper's presence passed through her, different from anything she'd felt before. Fragments of images flashed before her eyes. Lord Burgess speaking to a woman with long blond hair and green eyes. A dark cave filled with dragons and a shadowy figure. Dread washed over her, but she didn't know what it was from. And then there was searing pain. Mina gasped sharply and Copper's presence retreated.

She pulled her hand away from Lord Burgess and sat down, feeling weak and dizzy. The feeling quickly passed, and she turned her thoughts to Copper.

What did you see?

The scheme against Lord Klodian is true, he replied. *Does the name Kristofel D'Lance mean anything to you?*

Yes, he's the lord of the Dracan Dominion.

Lord and Lady Burgess work for him. He's plotting to overthrow the High Prince by making it seem that Lord Klodian and a man named Lord Culver are sowing rebellion. He wants to start a war.

So it is true, Mina said. *Before Vhan died, he said something about rumors of war. This must be what he was talking about. What else did you see?*

Many dark things that I cannot tell you yet. I must speak to my brethren and make sense of them first.

What should I do with him? If I leave him here, he'll starve to death. But I can't release him or he'll report back to Lord D'Lance.

I can erase his memories, Copper said. *It is not something to be done lightly, but the things I saw tell me this man is dangerous.*

Mina wavered in her decision for a moment. *Do it.*

She put her hand back on Lord Burgess's forehead and waited, but she didn't feel anything.

It is done.

That was fast, Mina replied. *What memories did you erase?*

Everything dealing with Lord D'Lance. The only thing he will remember is that he is loyal to Lord Klodian. Will that suffice, or should I create some new memories for him?

That should be fine. I'm going to release him and let the guards find him. He's not my problem after that. I need to tell Thais everything we've learned.

Don't forget the egg, Copper said.

I won't. I'll bring it to you tomorrow.

Very well. I will leave you now. I smell a storm coming.

Mina waited until she no longer felt the closeness of Copper's presence before she untied Lord Burgess. She pulled the gag from his mouth and leaned in close to him.

"You've been missing for an entire day," she said. "Lord Klodian has been looking all over for you. Tell the guards who you are and they will help you."

She stood and stuck her head out, glancing down the row of cells. There were no guards visible, so she sprinted to the door she'd entered through and escaped into the main hall. The room that held the egg was down here, she just had to figure out which one it was. She tried the handles of each one she passed and found they were all unlocked. Her luck couldn't get any better.

When Mina opened the third door on the left, she saw all sorts of trinkets. She stepped inside and walked around stacks of wooden crates filled with all manner of things. It appeared to be a storage room. She almost left, but a glint from one of the crates caught her eye. Mina removed a rug from the top of the crate and was rewarded.

The egg was inside.

But there was a problem. It was much larger than she remembered. How was she going to get it out of the castle without being seen, let alone up to her room? She stared at the egg for a long while as she pondered her options. It would be impossible to get it through the front gates without someone seeing her … unless she took it out there now. There were fewer prying eyes, but where would she hide it until she could deliver it to Copper?

This would require thinking on her feet. She pulled the egg from the crate and was surprised to find that it wasn't very heavy. She grabbed a cloak from another crate and used it to cover the egg, then peered into the hall to make sure it was still empty. All was clear, and she hurried up the stairs to the upper portion of the castle.

A few guards were making their rounds, but they didn't pay her any heed. She offered a prayer of thanks to Avera and reached the courtyard. The night air was cool, but it did little to ease her nervous sweating. Mina walked to the gates and stopped when she saw they were closed. Aram had told her they were being closed at night and she'd completely forgotten. She looked around the courtyard, but there was nowhere ideal to hide the egg.

Footsteps from behind her caused her to panic, but when she heard Thais's voice, she sighed with relief.

"What are you doing out here?"

"I need to hide this," Mina replied, lifting the cloak.

Thais's eyes widened. "Is that what I think it is?"

"What do you think it is?" Mina asked.

Thais locked eyes with her. "You said egg, and I didn't put it together. Gods, you *are* insane, aren't you? Lord Klodian will kill you if he finds out you've taken that."

"It was buried in a storage room, so I doubt he'll know it's missing for a while. Where can I put this? I'll get rid of it tomorrow."

"I have no idea," Thais said, glancing around.

"Can you get me outside the walls?"

"If I get caught doing this, I'll kill you. Follow me."

Thais led her to a side entrance and produced a ring of keys from her waist. She fumbled through them until she found the correct one, then unlocked the door. Mina stepped out into the open and set the egg down, then swiftly dug a hole in the sand with her hands. She kept the egg wrapped in the cloak and placed it in the hole, then covered it with sand. It wasn't perfect, but it would make due. She stepped back through the door and Thais locked it.

"We've got a problem," Mina said. "The High Prince is in danger."

22

After a few hours of fitful sleep, Caden got out of bed and prepared himself mentally for what lay ahead. He put on a chainmail shirt and strapped his sword at his waist, then headed to the bottom level of the barracks.

Angus was there, along with a contingent of Runesmen. They were all dressed for battle, and Caden looked questioningly at the commander.

"What's going on?"

"Lord Culver has attacked our settlements on the border, so Lord D'Lance has ordered me to go with you and your team to the front lines. The others will follow, but it's going to take some time to mobilize them."

Caden counted roughly thirty men, including himself and Angus. It certainly wasn't enough to defend against an army. His suspicion grew, but he kept his mouth shut. He needed to know the truth before he made his move.

"We should get moving, then," Caden said.

"You heard the captain. Mount up!"

The Runesmen filed out of the barracks to the stable where horses were already saddled and waiting for them. Caden chose a horse at random and climbed into the saddle. He waited until everyone was mounted, then he flicked the reins and guided the horse across the courtyard. Angus rode up beside him and they traveled side by side in silence for a long while.

"Lord D'Lance doesn't want to cause a panic, so we're to keep things nonchalant. Once we get past the surroundings towns, we'll need to pick up the pace."

"Yes, sir," Caden replied. "I've been wondering something …" He trailed off, waiting for Angus to press him.

"What is it?"

"Does Lord Culver employ banned magic?"

Angus subtly side-eyed him. "Who knows? The man is crazed with his lust for power. People like that are unpredictable. If he's using dark magic, it wouldn't surprise me."

"How else would someone create a fireball that can fly through the air at their command? That has to be magic, right?"

"Sounds like it to me."

Caden watched their surroundings with a critical eye, wondering what sort of ambush might be waiting for them. Burke's note told him not to trust anyone, but what about Angus? He was close to Lord D'Lance, that much was obvious, but was he aware of what his lord was plotting? And if he was, did he continue to follow the man out of loyalty, or fear? Caden decided it was too risky to say anything to the commander.

"We may be headed for trouble, then. I'm certain that Lord Culver has magic users in his arsenal. We have nothing to defend ourselves with against magic."

"Let us wait and see what lies ahead," Angus said. "It's possible the reports were exaggerated. At least, that's what I'm hoping. The last thing we need is a war on our hands."

If Angus was aware of Lord D'Lance's dealings, he played ignorant well. They continued along the dirt road, up and down hills, and eventually passed through the last sign of civilization for the next several miles.

"Time to speed things up!" Angus shouted.

His horse charged ahead. Caden urged his own mount, and soon they were thundering down the road at a break-neck pace. The scenery flashed by too quickly for him to take note of an ambush, so he kept his eyes on the road ahead. They rode as long as the horses could manage, then stopped to give them a water break. After a few minutes of rest, they were back on the road again.

It was late in the afternoon when they reached the border between the two Dominions. Caden slowed his horse down and surveyed the area. There was a walled city in the distance, on the other side of the border. It was surrounded by an open field of tall grass that swayed from a light breeze that had picked up.

"What is that place?" Caden asked.

"That's Yediff. It's one of Lord Culver's fortresses here on the border. He's got several of them."

"I don't see signs of an army."

"Neither do I, but we shouldn't let our guard down. They could be holed up in Yediff, waiting to attack."

Caden had a bad feeling in his gut. Something was wrong, just as it had been with Burke's death. He scanned the field, and though the grass was tall, it wasn't high enough to hide an army.

"What do you think we should do?"

Angus scratched his chin, his gaze glued to the city. "We should scout the area. I don't want the rest of our men walking into a trap with no escape." The commander turned his horse around to face the rest of the Runesmen.

"Split up and ride through the field. Look for anything out of the ordinary, but try not to draw attention to yourselves. If you find anything, alert the rest of us."

The men divided into pairs and rode across the border at a leisurely pace. Caden looked at Angus.

"I guess you're with me," he said, smiling.

"I guess so," Caden replied, flicking the reins.

The grass was golden yellow, and Caden realized it wasn't grass, but wheat. It stretched as far as he could see, and aside from Yediff, there was nothing else around.

"They've got plenty of crops," he muttered.

"The Toren Dominion has lots of ideal farmland," Angus said. "It's one of the reasons Lord Culver has gained his wealth. He exports the excess food to his neighbors."

"Everyone has to eat."

"Indeed."

Caden continued to search for signs of an army or even the presence of one that might have passed through, but there was nothing that caught his eye. He wondered for a brief moment if he was being paranoid about Lord D'Lance, but he quickly reminded himself of all the evidence contrary to that thought.

As they neared Yediff, he scanned the wall for guards. There were none that he could see, and he found it curious.

"If Lord Culver is encroaching on the Dracan Dominion, I'd assume this place would be crawling with his troops."

"Maybe it was a diversion," Angus replied. "Perhaps the real attack is coming from somewhere else."

Something heavy struck Caden in the back of the head and he fell out of the saddle, crashing hard on the ground face-first. He rolled onto his back, and the world spun around him. His headache returned with a vengeance. Angus slid out of the saddle and came to stand over him.

"What happened?" Caden asked, confused.

"You shouldn't have gone snooping, you blasted fool. Burke should have kept his mouth shut. It would have saved *your* life, at least."

"Burke's death wasn't an accident, was it?" Caden's vision returned to normal, and he reached for the hilt of his sword. Angus kicked his hand aside and pressed his foot onto Caden's chest, then unsheathed his own sword.

"Don't bother fighting," Angus warned. "You're a dead man either way."

23

"I thought Lord Klodian was the one in danger?" Thais asked.

"He is, too, but Lord Burgess was part of a bigger plot."

"Was?" Thais's face paled. "Is he dead?"

"No," Mina shook her head. She didn't know how to explain things without revealing everything that had happened with Copper. She wished Caden was here, but there was no changing that now. She would have to trust Thais, as much as it went against her instincts.

"I want you to swear that you won't repeat what I'm about to tell you."

"Won't repeat it to who?"

"Anyone. This stays between us."

Thais eyed her distrustfully. "Did you kill someone?"

"Don't be absurd. Just promise me before I change my mind. I'm offering to trust you with something."

"You don't have to be dramatic. I won't say anything."

Mina took a deep breath. "Dragons can talk."

Thais's left eye twitched, but she didn't say

anything.

"I know it sounds crazy, but—"

"I believe you."

"—just listen … what?"

"I said I believe you."

They stared at each other in silence for a moment.

"You do?" Mina asked.

Thais nodded.

"Why?"

"I have my reasons. What does that have to do with the High Prince?"

Mina told Thais everything beginning with her talk with Copper on the mesa before the sand wyrm showed up to their interrogation in the dungeon. Thais listened intently and didn't seem to be surprised by any of it. Mina related most of the details but left out the part of being bonded to a dragon and the bit of history that Copper had told her.

"Should we tell Lord Klodian?"

"No," Thais answered almost immediately. "At least, not yet. We need to eliminate Lady Burgess before she reports to back to Lord D'Lance if she hasn't already."

"You don't mean kill her?"

"No, not if we can help it. Can your dragon

friend erase her memory as well?"

"I can ask him," Mina said.

"After she's dealt with, we can take all of this to Captain Eduard."

"Can he be trusted? We saw him talking in secret with Lord Burgess."

"I don't think the captain is a traitor. He has access to Lord Klodian at all hours of the day. If he wanted to do something, he'd have done it by now."

Mina silently conceded the point. She didn't know Eduard very well, but she had decided to trust Thais, which meant that she needed to be confident in the woman's judgment.

"What if he doesn't believe us? If Lady Burgess's memories are erased, then neither one of them can attest to Lord D'Lance's plan."

"Then as one of Lord Klodian's advisors, you can tell him directly."

Mina didn't know if he would believe her wild tale, but as long as she told him, her conscience would be clear. She nodded.

"What do you plan on doing with that egg?" Thais asked.

"I'm taking it back where it belongs."

"To the dragons. Makes sense, but is it safe? What if you hand it over and the dragon eats you?"

"He won't," Mina replied.

Thais shrugged. "If you say so. What about that

wyrm thing? Is it still out there?"

"I don't know. I didn't ask Copper if he killed it."

"Copper, huh? So they have names?"

"Yes. They aren't mindless animals at all. Everything we've ever thought about them might be wrong."

"What changed your opinion about them?"

The question gave Mina pause. She honestly didn't have a clear answer. She supposed it was lots of little things all tied together.

"I guess Copper changed my mind about them," she said. "It's difficult to explain."

Thais remained silent, but Mina thought the woman looked like she wanted to say something. She waited, but Thais didn't speak.

"Say it."

"Say what?"

"Whatever is on your mind," Mina said.

"I suppose I'm feeling guilty."

"About what?"

Thais sighed. "You're forced to trust me because you need my help. I shouldn't feel obligated, but I do. For the record, I don't enjoy the feeling. I've never relied on anyone before, and I don't expect to in the future."

Mina frowned, confused. "I don't understand

whatever it is you're trying to say."

"I'll ask the same promise of you. What I'm going to say could get me killed by many different people."

"You can trust me."

Although they were the only two people present, Thais lowered her voice.

"I believe you about the dragons because I've seen it myself."

"You've seen me talking with Copper?"

"No. I've seen what Lord D'Lance is doing. I tried to tell Caden when he was here, but he said I was crazy."

Mina was more confused than before. She opened her mouth to say something, then pursed her lips.

"He didn't tell you?" Thais asked.

"If he did, I must have missed it."

"The attack on Slia was done by dragons, but it wasn't an accident. Lord D'Lance was behind it. He's a wicked man, and the things he's doing are evil. He found a way to unite humans and dragons, but it isn't natural."

"What do you mean 'unite?'"

"He's using dark magic to force dragons into some sort of bond with humans. They can share each other's thoughts and communicate telepathically. Slia was a test. He wanted to see how his creation would work as a weapon."

Mina remembered what Copper had said about how humans and dragons had once been allies, and about the bond they shared. Had Lord D'Lance learned of it somehow and tried to recreate it by force? She would have to tell Copper.

"So Lord D'Lance attacked Slia with dragons? How can he control them?"

"His soldiers control them through their bond. They are magically bound to follow their rider's commands."

"The soldiers ride the dragons?" Mina asked.

"Yes, and Lord D'Lance is building an army of them. He's going to use them to take the throne from the High Prince."

Things were starting to make sense to Mina. Lord Burgess's mission to overthrow Klodian was part of the bigger picture, and Lord D'Lance's ultimate goal was to take over as High Prince. He needed something to divert attention from himself, and making Klodian and Lord Culver appear to be forming a rebellion was the diversion. There was one thing she didn't understand.

"How do you know all this?"

"Lord D'Lance sent me here … as a spy."

24

Caden stared up at Angus, angry with himself for not being more vigilant.

"You could let me go. I won't come back to the Dracan. I'll go to my grave with what I know." He doubted the commander would believe his words. Caden glanced to his horse. If he could get on his feet quickly enough, he was confident he could reach the mount and get to the city before Angus could catch him.

"Lord D'Lance doesn't want to any loose ends. So long as you live, you pose a threat. But I'm not the one you need to beg. It's not my blade that will be your end."

Angus removed his foot and drove his sword down, stabbing the point through Caden's chainmail and into the ground, pinning him in place. They locked eyes, and Caden prayed the man would help him, but Angus turned away and mounted his horse. He grabbed the reins of Caden's horse and rode back across the border.

Caden struggled to pull the sword free, but the angle was awkward and he couldn't get the leverage he needed.

"Help!" He cried out.

Did the other Runesmen know what was happening? Would they come to his aid, or had they left him there to die? He continued struggling and eventually, the sword loosened enough that he was able to get up. Caden ran for the city, waving his arms around. The closer he got to the walls of the city, the more his eyes began to play tricks on him.

The stone rippled like water, and when he reached the gate, he passed right through it. The city was an illusion. It faded before his eyes, leaving only a black cloud behind. Caden spun around, looking in every direction. There was nothing but the expanse of wheat fields. A whistling sound filled the air, and he turned to look at the cloud. It was swirling and began to expand in a circle, leaving a hole in the middle.

Caden watched the cloud with uncertainty, knowing it was the product of magic but scared of what it might do. The cloud continued stretching until it encircled a large portion of the field, then it touched the ground and the wheat erupted in flames. The fire spread quickly, and Caden realized too late what was happening.

He looked to the border and saw Angus, along with a robed figure who was directing the cloud with his hands. Caden couldn't see the man's face, but he knew it was Lord D'Lance. He must have found out that Burke had discovered what he was doing, and once he knew that Caden was also involved, it only made sense that the Dominion Lord would want him dead, too.

Ash and gray smoke billowed into the sky, blotting out the landscape and obscuring his view. Caden knew he needed to warn Lord Culver and the High Prince, but if he burned to death here, the

Dominions would end up engulfed in war. He jogged along the perimeter, looking for a spot where he could get through the flames unscathed. Unfortunately, the fires burned intensely and the heat drove him back.

As the flames consumed everything in their path, Caden's hope began to flee. There was no way to escape. He was going to die, burned alive. All of his dreams and ambitions flashed within his mind, and he cursed Lord D'Lance as a fool and a coward. He kept moving despite the knowledge that this was the end. The wind blew the smoke into his face, and he coughed, covering his mouth with the crook of his arm.

Something whizzed through the air, striking the ground beside him. Through blurry eyes, he saw it was an arrow. Another one struck the ground a few away from the first one, and another. The smoke was too thick for him to see anything, and he gasped in surprise when an arrow struck him in the chest. It pierced his chainmail shirt and cut through his flesh, hitting bone.

Caden slumped to the ground on his knees, clutching the arrow. He wanted to pull it out, but he knew it didn't matter if he did. Nothing mattered anymore. He saw more arrows zip through the smoke, but they missed him. Breathing became difficult, though whether it was the smoke or his wound, he didn't know.

He struggled to stay up, but his vision was spinning. Caden felt himself falling, and then he was on his back, staring up at the gray sky.

Darkness began to fill the edges of his vision, and it slowly dawned on him that it wasn't the lack of sunlight. This was it. His life was slipping away. He pictured Mina in his mind and prayed that she wasn't mad at him for the kiss they'd shared.

The darkness beckoned him, and he followed it. As the shroud of death closed around him, he thought he heard a woman's voice calling his name.

Caden ... come to me ...

25

The next morning, Mina lay awake in her bed, thinking about everything Thais had told her the night before. The woman had been forced into working for Lord D'Lance because he had her parents as captives. Mina considered telling Lord Klodian everything, but she knew it would lead to him asking questions that she wouldn't be able to answer, not without endangering Copper.

She forced herself out of bed, yawning and stretching. She was tired, but she wanted to get the egg to Copper as soon as possible. The only problem she faced was how to carry it. Due to its size, it would be difficult to transport on horseback, and she didn't want to go on foot. Mina mulled it over as she got dressed, then headed down to the dining hall and ate a quick meal.

While she was eating, she saw one of the servants carrying a baby. It was swaddled in a cloth that was wrapped around the woman's body, giving her the ability to use her hands. That gave her an idea, and she went to Klodian's seamstress and got a long swath of cloth cut. The seamstress waved away her money, telling her that Lord Klodian's advisors didn't have to pay.

It still felt odd for her to be in a position of privilege. She rolled the cloth up and went to the stable. Aram was working again, and he gave her a look that told her he wasn't happy to see her.

"If you're here for a horse, you'll have to take Vesper. Tempest has been taken already."

Mina was disappointed to hear that, but she nodded. "Very well."

Vesper was similar in size to Tempest, but he was a chestnut color and seemed temperamental. Aram struggled to saddle the horse, and once he was done, he handed Mina the reins.

"Good luck with this one," he muttered.

Mina led the horse out of the gate on foot and went to where she'd buried the egg. She was relieved to see it was still there. Unrolling the cloth she'd got, she placed the egg in the center and wrapped it, then wound the cloth around her upper body, cinching it tightly. It seemed firmly in place, but she jumped a few times to make sure. Satisfied it wouldn't come loose, she climbed into the saddle and guided Vesper into the desert.

As they approached the mesa, she looked for the body of the sand wyrm, but there was no sign of it. Mina wondered if the dragons had eaten it, but guessed that might not be the case as there were no bones left behind. She could feel that Copper wasn't on the mesa. His presence was still pulsing from the scale, but he seemed far away.

She guessed he was with his brethren, and so she left the horse at the base of the mesa and climbed her way to the top. It was more difficult than her first venture, mainly because of the added weight of the egg. Once she was safe atop the mesa, she untied the cloth and removed the egg, setting it down on the ground. Its surface was scaled like a dragon's, but the scales were smaller and more closely overlapped.

The color had dulled since the last time she'd seen it. It had once been copper like the scale in her leg, but now it was a light blueish-green. Mina looked over the edge of the mesa and admired the view. The desert was a harsh place, but it was also beautiful. Some people found comfort among the busy city streets, but not Mina. She enjoyed the peace that nature brought.

After an hour of walking around the mesa, she heard the flapping of wings and looked to the sky. Copper was swiftly approaching. She hurried back to the egg and waited for him to land. He swooped down and touched the ground on the other side of the mesa, then folded his wings behind him and walked over to where she waited.

You were successful this time, he said.

I was.

Mina lifted the egg and carried it to the dragon, placing it at his feet. Copper leaned down and inspected it, and Mina caught the scent of orchids. She tilted her head curiously.

What is it?

This egg will never hatch.

Mina's heart sank. *It's dead?*

Not completely, but there is not enough life in it to survive. Even now I can feel it slowly fading.

I'm sorry.

It is the way of life sometimes, Copper said. *Regardless, I am glad it has been returned to us. I spoke to my brethren about the things I saw in Lord Burgess's mind last night, and we are in agreement that what this Lord D'Lance has done is a perversion and must be stopped.*

Thais told me that he's forcing humans and dragons to bond using magic.

How does she know this?

It's a long story, but she has seen it with her own eyes. She said Lord D'Lance is building an army to use against the High Prince. He wants the throne for himself.

Copper growled. *What we sought to prevent is unfolding before us again. Perhaps we were wrong in our thinking. Perhaps humans will never stop.*

We aren't all bad, Mina said.

Copper regarded her in silence. *No, not all,* he said. *Yet those that are always seem to wield power. And they always want more of it. Humans do not know how to be content. I fear the time has come that dragons must wage war against the darkness.*

War? Do you really think it will come to that?

Yes.

A war between humans and dragons would be disastrous. There must be another way.

I'm afraid there isn't. The elders have already made their decision. They are making preparations even as we speak.

Innocent people will be caught in the middle, Mina protested. *Please, you must ask them to reconsider. If we can find a way to stop Lord D'Lance and free the dragons from the magic, that should be enough, shouldn't it?*

You are asking me to go against the stream, he said. *The elders have grown tired of seeing dragons killed, and what Lord D'Lance has done has pushed them over the edge.*

Then let me speak to them. Mina didn't know why she said those words. They just slipped right out of her mouth. She stared up at Copper, silently praying he would deny her.

There is much you will need to learn about being bonded to a dragon. As a bonded human, you are allowed certain privileges, such as an audience before the elders. I will take you to them, but I cannot guarantee they will heed your words.

Although she was afraid, Mina knew that she was probably the only person who might be bonded to a dragon. At least, not forcibly. If she could avert a war between their two races, then certainly she had to try.

I wish to speak with them, even if they won't listen.

Very well. It is a long journey from here, and we will go deep into the desert where it is not safe for you, but I will do my best to protect you. We will need to go now, else we may be too late.

Now? Mina's eyes widened. *But I'm not ready to go yet.*

In this matter, time is not on our side. If we don't go now, then war will come.

Mina looked over her shoulder in the direction of the castle. She couldn't see it from here, but she knew it was there in the distance. Why had she suddenly been thrust into the middle of this? It was partly because she didn't know how to keep her mouth shut, true, but she was a nobody. Who would listen to what she had to say?

You have more worth than you give yourself credit for, Copper said.

That's hard to believe when you've spent your entire life being told differently.

Perhaps, but the opinions of others should not influence how you view yourself.

She knew he was right, but that didn't change her mental struggle. Either way, her view of her worth wasn't important right now. There were much larger things at play, things that she potentially had the chance to sway.

If we must go now, then so be it.

Copper hummed in satisfaction and lowered himself close to the ground.

Climb upon my back, he said.

Truly?

Unless you want to go in my claws, but that will not be comfortable. Riding upon my back is one of the benefits I mentioned.

Mina took a few hesitant steps, then steeled her mind against her fears. She climbed up Copper's shoulder and sat upon his back, hardly believing that it was all real. Copper grabbed the egg in his mouth and flexed his wings out.

Hold on, he warned her.

She dug her fingers under the scales on Copper's neck and closed her eyes. Her stomach flipped and turned as she felt herself falling, and then the sensation was gone. She peeked her eyes open and saw they were flying above the mesas. It was both exhilarating and terrifying. Copper turned south, and the desert stretched as far as she could see.

I'm afraid, Mina said.

I know, Copper replied.

They continued over the landscape, toward the elders, the possibility of war, and many other things yet to be seen.

But mostly, Mina knew they were headed toward the unknown.

THE END OF BOOK TWO

ABOUT THE AUTHOR

Richard Fierce is a fantasy and space opera author. He's been writing since childhood, but began publishing in 2007. Since then, he's written multiple novels and short stories.

In 2000, Richard won Poet of the Year for his poem *The Darkness*. He's also one of the creative brains behind the Allatoona Book Festival, a literary event in Acworth, Georgia.

A recovering retail worker, he now works in the tech industry when he's not busy writing.

He's married and has three step-daughters (pray for him), a grandson, three dogs (huskies!), four cats, and two ferrets. He basically has a zoo.

His love affair with fantasy was born in high school when a friend's mother gave him a copy of *Dragons of Spring Dawning* by Margaret Weis and Tracy Hickman.